I0452540

Alice Dippleblack in

Training

Days

By
K. J. Bailey

Second Edition

This is a work of fiction. Names, characters, places, and incidents either are the products of the author's imagination or are used fictitiously. Any resemblance to actual persons, living or dead, businesses, companies, events, or locales is entirely coincidental.

ISBN: 978-0-9978858-4-2

Chapter 1

Farms and Orchards

Alice brings down her broadsword, Jellybane, on another of the forearm length grasshoppers, bisecting it before it can hop away again. She then picks up the still moving yellow and red body, dropping it in her sack with a dozen or so others before looking for more.

She hears Danahlia counting happily, "Eighteen," as the Liguna manages to skewer another elsewhere in the corn field. The lizard girl then amends, "Feventheen." It sounds muffled like her mouth is full.

The corn stalks are impressively tall, well over Alice's head, blocking her view, but have been planted in neat rows, giving her enough room to move through them. She spots another one of the invading bugs about mid-way up another stalk, busily devouring a leaf. She slaps it to the ground with the flat of her blade, doing her best not to damage the plant itself, before chasing after the now dizzily hopping insect.

Alice Dippleblack is a young Tokala of fourteen. She shares many features with her fox cousins, including her face, fur, and tail. Though she, unlike her feral counterparts, walks on two legs. Her coat is a fine orange red, the color of late sunsets, save for the black tips of her triangular ears, nose, hands, and feet. The very tip of her full fluffy tail is white, the same color as her countershading, which starts at her lower lip, runs back to round her cheeks and then travels down her neck and into her graying blouse. She wears brown trousers and runs barepaw on the soft earth.

It's been a few weeks since the battle at the forest stream with the Order of Thermathrogi's agent. In the time since, the girls have made their way through the forest to a choice bit of open country consisting of wide open plains, a few small villages, and a handful of secluded farms. They're taking a break from their journey now at a farm they found to be sympathetic to the plight of Cold Bloods like Danahlia. It's run by an elderly Bovidan couple who, despite their advanced years, have managed to grow enough to feed themselves and occasionally trade in local markets. It had rained quite a bit in the area over the last two weeks, and what had seemed a blessing now brought a plague.

After the rains encouraged some last minute growth in the nearly ripe corn, a swarm of grasshoppers had descended upon the farm's fields. Alice, Danahlia, and Twinkaleni, have thus offered their services as monster hunters to help rid the crop of the pests as payment for being allowed to rest there. They'd been at it for several days now but the afflicted fields are vast and the insects' numbers great. Even so, the young fox girl runs down the grasshoppers with enthusiasm, invigorated with all the training the trio is getting in.

As a result of them all nearly being killed by a single agent of the dreadful Order, only surviving because of the heroic sacrifice of a dear friend, Twinkaleni continually insists that they need to train. To Alice and Danahlia, training has mostly been a game to enjoy and pass the time, whether it was sparring, running races, and now, vanquishing big bugs. Twinkaleni, however, has taken her training very seriously, working on improving her body as well as her mind. Twinkaleni is a Murin. Her mouse-like features along with her diminutive stature and abnormally large round ears make the light gray furred twelve year old look terribly cute. None the less, the youngest of the trio possesses incredible magical powers.

She demonstrates this now with a call of "Feasta!" and before Alice's eyes, the grasshopper she chases is hit with a wrist thick beam of fire that washes over it. It lasts only a second, but the insect sizzles and pops under the intense heat, charred black as it falls to its side, smoking.

Alice, unable to stop her momentum, has to leap over it and cries, "Hey, that was mine."

"Mm, there are plenty to go around, I'm sure," says Twinkaleni without inflection, already scanning for others.

A small Bovidan boy, the grandson of the elderly couple, whoops in delight as he follows the mage around to watch her impressive displays, as well as to collect her fallen foes. Alice frowns as the young cow boy gathers up the charred bug with the end of his shirt before tossing it into his own burlap sack.

Ever since the battle with the Order, the Murin had changed. Alice had never known her to be an overly playful sort, but now she was being downright dour. Even Danahlia had almost entirely stopped good naturedly teasing her. The mouse mage had also begun using her magic rather liberally, sometimes bordering on reckless. Though she hadn't ever intentionally harmed her companions, there had been a few close calls, and these she would justify like all the others by claiming it was crucial training.

The training was to help make good on a vow the tiny Murin had made to bring down the Order that had ruined her life, as well as ended the lives of many innocent children that the girls had known for too short a time but had still come to care for. One of which, a Lobovan named Lyca, had saved their lives at the cost of her own. Since then, Twinkaleni Orbear had been doing all she could to push herself to new heights of physical and magical power. Not willing to let her go it alone, Danahlia and Alice support her as much as they can, agreeing it will be a good thing to get themselves into shape as well.

It's already late in the day and after a couple more hours bug hunting, a bell is rung to call everyone back to the farmhouse for supper. As she approaches the simple thatch roofed dwelling, she meets up with Danahlia who asks how many grasshoppers she caught.

"Twenty-eight," Alice states proudly.

"Not bad, for a bushy tailed trainee," Danahlia says haughtily, dumping out her sack so her haul can be sorted, "But the real monster hunter got twenty-nine."

"Hm, looks like twenty-seven here," says the old farmer, seated on a wooden crate beside the fire set before the house.

"Ha!" Alice barks as Danahlia kneels down to count again.

"No way, I remember gettin' twenty nine, I know I did," Danahlia counters, shifting around her catch with clawed fingers. Danahlia Smoothide is a Liguna, a race with features similar to lizards though she walks and talks just as Alice does. Her skin is completely furless with a color and pattern like oak tree bark, though very smooth to the touch. She is two years older and a bit taller than Alice, even while hunching, and has a lithe, well-proportioned body with long slender limbs and a lengthy tail that now swished behind her as she counts the bugs she caught for a third time.

"Huh, I guess some of 'em got away," she says, standing back up with a frown.

Alice grins, poking a finger at the corner of Danahlia's mouth, where a grasshopper's transparent wing is sticking out, "I bet."

Danahlia pulls it away and looks at it before smiling sheepishly, "Oh yeah."

Alice shakes her head before dumping her haul atop Danahlia's. Twinkaleni and the small cow boy join them and all the bugs are sorted based on how intact they are. Years of hard living have taught the Bovidan farmers how to make the best of a bad situation, and the insects are placed in piles atop beds of corn leaves to be cooked and otherwise eaten. Those that are too badly damaged will be tossed around the corn for fertilizer, those slightly less so will be fed to the ferals the farmers keep, while the grasshoppers that are relatively intact will be placed over the fire and baked into crispy treats.

While they sort, the Farmer's wife emerges from the house with mugs of water for everyone. She is a kind, heavy set Bovidan with a white coat and light brown splotches. As she hands her thinner, mostly brown coated, husband a mug, they rub noses, sharing a smile in an adorable ritual that looks as old and comfortable as they are. Their little, white and black splotched grandson, Dumi, sticks his tongue out in disgust at the affectionate display before prattling on to his elders about the incredible feats of magic he witnessed throughout the day.

Alice quenches her thirst and watches the bugs cook, skewered over the fire. They don't take long at all and are soon served wrapped in a corn leaf. Danahlia couldn't care less if they're cooked or not and crunches on raw and fire roasted bugs alike. Alice and Twinkaleni, however, prefer them seared to a fine crisp. Alice doesn't care much for the chitinous front half of the insects, which are much too rigid for her taste. Rather, she pulls them apart, tossing the front half into the animal feed pile and eating the much fleshier abdomen. That, she's discovered, is where the flavor is.

Little wisps of steam plume from the broken bugs, revealing pale yellow flesh. Alice blows on these before biting into them. The outer chitin has crunch but little flavor, while the meat reminds her of the crab she and her friends had back in the pixie forest in both flavor and texture. The bugs are really quite appetizing, making it unfortunate that they went bad so quickly. Only after a few hours to a day, they begin to take on a sour flavor that grew stronger until they were utterly inedible. But on the bright side, this did give everyone a good excuse to gluttonously eat their fill while they were still good.

After a few bugs, the elderly farmer rises to feed the feral animals he keeps. Alice, Twinkaleni, and Dumi join him in taking up the leftover and crushed up insects to the various pens the ferals are kept in, though Danahlia is far too occupied with eating to be bothered with the task. The first is a small fenced enclosure with several chickens, some white and a few brown. Their pen is made up of sticks held with bits of twine. It looks fairly flimsy but the chickens seem content to stay in it, gathering as they see the farmer approach.

Alice liked feeding the ferals, watching them wander around their pens, listening to the noises they made, and sometimes petting them. These chickens weren't like the ones she had seen tucked in tiny cages at Carton's market some weeks ago. The dozen or so fowl on the farm were free to walk about their pen and even had a little house in which to take refuge and lay eggs in, which they did nearly every morning. The farmer showed the girls how the eggs needed to be cleaned and then where boiled in water from a well on the property. The eggs were delicious and Alice made a point of thanking the chickens for them. They now toss handfuls of grasshopper into the pen and watch as the chickens fall over them, clucking happily as they pick and peck at the pieces.

The next pen they visit is a much larger, more open, enclosure, home to three cows and a large draft horse. Alice didn't think such animals would be interested in grasshoppers but they eagerly gather to eat what the farmer offers them. He says they don't get much protein from what they normally eat, so this is a rare opportunity. Alice holds out a few legs and crushed bug bits as she sees the Bovidan do and one of the cows comes to eat from her hand. It's an unusual sensation, warm and sloppy, but wonderfully fulfilling at the same time as the cow licks and munches her offering. Alice looks to Twinkaleni, who grins back but hasn't tried feeding the large animals herself yet.

Slowly, as she had done the day before, Alice reaches out with her other hand until she can feel the jaw of the cow working on the pieces of bug. Gently, with the very tips of her fingers, she strokes the animal's muzzle up to its cheek, and when it doesn't pull away she rests her hand on it to give it a pet. Once the cow has licked her hand clean it starts to nudge her palm with its nose and makes a little grunt. Alice gets more grasshopper and that seems to satisfy it. She motions for Twinkaleni to come closer, but the little Murin just grins and shakes her head.

The massive draft mare walks over to investigate Alice, its large head coming to hang over the top of the fence to sniff at her. She can feel the horse's warm breath on her ears and it makes them twitch, but when she lifts a hand to pet it, the mare steps away with a little whinny. Without a word, the Bovidan farmer puts some more bug bits in her hand and lifts it up to the mare. Tentatively, the great horse comes back and after a few sniffs, begins eating from her palm. Alice has to force herself to keep from bursting with joy, this was the first time the horse ate from her hand. Instead, she manages a wide grin, the farmer nodding his approval.

The girls stay on the farm for only a few more days until the swarm of grasshoppers dwindles. The Bovidans insist they could stay for a while longer and help bring in the harvest, but upon hearing that neighbors would be coming to lend a hand as well, Twinkaleni convinces her companions it would be wise to leave. They bid their farewells to the kind Bovidans to resume their journey. The cow people gave each of them some corn, which was just becoming ripe and tasted sweet even raw. They also received a few water skins worth of fresh milk from the feral cows. They had some while at the farm and knew it was delicious.

With the ongoing Blood War, a conflict between the warm and cold blooded races, all the lands of Arsalia were dangerous for cold blooded people like Danahlia. Thus, the fewer people who saw her, the better. It was fortunate though, that as the trio travel the country, they find many sympathetic to the Cold Bloods stranded on the wrong side of the battle lines. Before the war had begun, both the warm and cold blooded got along in relative harmony, freely traveling, trading, and living with each other. But as the fires of war caught, old hatreds and paranoia spread throughout the kingdom. Now, the borders between Cold and Warm Blood territory have become vicious battlegrounds fought over by vast armies, making travel between the nations perilous. As such, the Cold Bloods trapped in Warm Blood territory had to do their best to conceal their identities in the hopes that they could sneak back to their people or, like Danahlia planned to, wait out the war.

The less populated country side, furthest from the conflict, seems least affected by it. True, farms lacked for laborers and even then had to give a larger share of their crops to help the war effort, but other than that, life was little changed out here. The peace preceding the war had let many bonds of friendship bloom between the different peoples. Some of these bonds endure even in these troubled times, encouraging some to aid the stranded Cold Bloods when they can by offering food and shelter.

Heavily populated areas such as towns and cities were considerably more dangerous. More people meant an increased chance of encounters with those who had personal prejudices against Danahlia's kind or have been swept up in the propaganda and newly instituted laws claiming Cold Bloods as an enemy people. Just having such individuals around meant that those who would normally offer aid were at risk of being accused of treason. This alone tended to deter many from helping, even though they themselves had no qualms with the cold blooded. Thus as a rule, the girls have been avoiding larger settlements as much as they could.

They walk through wide open plains, keeping off larger roads in favor of less traveled paths. Alice and Twinkaleni would scout out potential resting places while Danahlia stayed hidden until their return. They find many orchards, ranches, and farms are welcoming of Danahlia, either because they are sympathetic to her plight or simply needed the extra help during harvest time, though more likely a mix of both. It was early fall now and all sorts of crops were beginning to ripen, meaning there was no shortage of work to be done.

As with the Bovidan's corn fields, many other crops were attracting unwanted attention, as now more than ever, the harvest was slow to be brought in. Whether it was frantically picking produce or fending off crop devouring invaders, the girls' services are in great demand. With most of the men, and even many of the boys, drafted into military service, all those that were left to tend the fields were the elderly, the women, and the children. This left much work to be done by fewer and less experienced hands. But to the trio's favor, it also made people especially grateful for any help, which rarely left the girls wanting for food or a place to rest.

With their rare skills and arms, the girls are often tasked with fending off all manner of hungry creatures, intent on making easy meals of the various farmers' hard labor. One apple orchard suffered from unusually long necked ferals that came out of a nearby wood at night to dine on the ripe fruit. The orchard had a fence erected around much of it, but the Ariokey, as the orchardists called them, have powerful legs that would let them leap clear over it. The Echanian woman, who ran the orchard, and her four daughters would pick during the day while the trio would keep look out among the trees at night. Previous, the horse people would try to do both but were often overwhelmed and left exhausted.

The arrangement worked well and more apples could be picked, eaten, sold, or made into various pies and treats, which were generously shared. It also gave the girls the opportunity to train with the bow Lyca had given them. The monster hunters had made arrows along their travels using the straightest sticks they could find for shafts and feathers from birds they managed to bring down. They were a little crude and without proper heads but occasionally proved effective.

While on watch during the night among the apple trees, the girls would hear the approach of the beasts and Twinkaleni would call forth her starlight spell with a shout of "Estraleete!" Startled by the noise and sudden illumination, the Ariokey would freeze in place, giving either Danahlia or Alice a chance to loose a few arrows. Twinkaleni lacked the arm span to draw the bow to any strength so its use was always up to the taller girls.

They had brought a couple of the animals down in this fashion over the course of their stay and feasted on fresh apple sweetened meat. This was rather rare however. With the Echanians preferring their apples, the girls didn't kill more than they wished to eat themselves and on most nights when Twinkaleni surprised the beasts, they would simply shout and run at the creatures to scare them off.

On another orchard, this one growing several types of berries, the trio was tasked with keeping away large, plump, nearly flightless, brown birds that would ravage the berry bushes at every opportunity. The Lotarins that kept the orchard called them ground rails and were often forced from their berry picking to chase the ravenous birds off with sticks. The birds came around during the morning most often and the girls managed to bring a few down with arrows. They found not only their meat to be good but their feathers were long and made for excellent fletching.

While venturing out to a nearby thicket in search of more potential arrow shafts, the girls discovered the area to be where a few of the birds had chosen to nest. The ground rails made large bowl shaped nests from reeds and twigs nestled among tall grasses. Once the birds where scared away, the girls raided them for their great eggs, usually only one per nest, and brought them back to eat. Alice had mixed feelings about this, but Danahlia assured her that the birds would just make new nests elsewhere, hopefully far from the raccoon people's berries. Grateful, the Lotarin family let the girls stay as long as they pleased and together they shared many feasts of ground rails dressed with berry sauces.

Leaving the orchard loaded with berries and bird meat, the girls travel on in a northerly direction across a vast plain thick with long grass and bushes but few trees. The ground is soft, the air warm, and the breeze cool, making for a pleasant walk. With no particular destination in mind, they wander late into the afternoon until Twinkaleni suggests they prepare camp and get in some sparring before it becomes too late. Danahlia and Alice have little interest in this, but the tiny Murin insists it is to their benefit.

Laying their packs and other gear in a pile, they each retrieve the sticks they have come to carry with them for their practice bouts. Danahlia has the longest, which stands in for her spear, while Alice has a middle size stick to replace her sword. Twinkaleni pulls free two small sticks from her pack which she wields in place of the two knives she uses, or at least intends to use, in battle, if it ever comes to it.

At first they have a free for all, Alice and Danahlia clashing playfully while Twinkaleni tries to cut in. After a short while, the Murin mage tries to face the other girls one on one. However, despite improvement, the small mouse struggles to overcome the taller girls. She uses no magic in these matches, relying instead on her somewhat unimpressive physical abilities. Twinkaleni tries hard, coming up with new attack patterns that have Alice and Danahlia needing to adapt, but her small size and lack of reach prove extremely frustrating obstacles for her. Alice is swift and twice her size, while Danahlia is even taller and has great reach with her long stick. Try as she might, Twinkaleni simply can't get near enough to land any hits.

The tiny mouse gets careless in her desire to land at least one strike and leaves herself open to a bop on the head from Alice's stick. With a pained squeak, she drops her weapons, instinctively reaching up for the throbbing spot just between her ears.

Immediately dropping her own stick, Alice falls to her knees beside the Murin, "Oh ticks, I'm sorry, Twinkaleni. I didn't mean to..."

"It's alright," the Murin winces, tears in her eyes and breathless, "Well struck, Alice."

The Tokala pulls away the mouse girl's tiny hands, "Here, let me see." Twinkaleni lets her and after pushing aside some light gray fur, Alice finds a bright pink bump on the smaller girl's normally paler skin. "Oh, geez, I'm so sorry," she apologizes again.

"I think that's enough practice for today," says Danahlia, leaning in over them to see.

"I want, to keep going," says Twinkaleni, breathing hard and picking her sticks back up.

Danahlia shakes her head, "No, it's gettin' late and I'm tired."

The Murin steps away from the fox girl, "Very well. Once more then, Alice."

"Uh, I think we should stop too," Alice says, slow to retrieve her training weapon.

"Come now, we can't call it quits just because of this," Twinkaleni complains, pointing up to her head.

"I said that's enough. Now let's eat," Danahlia orders. Standing over her backpack, the Liguna tosses down her staff and starts rummaging for food.

"But we must get stronger!" Twinkaleni cries angrily.

"And we will, "Danahlia assures her, "Just not anymore today. Not like we have a time limit to bring down that order."

"But we do, Danny!" Twinkaleni insists.

"What? Why?" asks Alice.

"While the Blood War rages the Order is vulnerable, less heavily guarded and hastily managed! If peace returns before it falls, we will have no hope of seeing to its ruin!"

"And what hope do we have now?" counters Danahlia, pulling free a leaf wrapped drumstick from her pack and sitting down.

"Little, but at least a chance," Twinkaleni affirms.

Alice joins Danahlia in freeing some dinner from their stores, "You seriously want to attack the Order?"

"Do you not?!" exclaims Twinkaleni, flabbergasted, "Have you already forgotten what they did to Lyca, Philip, Nesu, and all the forest children?!"

"No, I haven't," Alice nearly growls, insulted by the idea that she would ever forget the loss of their friends. "But I also haven't forgotten that just *one* of their people nearly killed us, did kill Lyca, even when we all faced 'im together! And you want us to attack a whole building full of 'em?!" says Alice, unable to help working up to a shout.

Danahlia nods enthusiastically, hooking a thumb at Alice, her mouth already full. Twinkaleni frowns, turning away. She then takes several steps and sits with her back to them.

Alice sighs, abandoning her pack to walk over to her, "I'm sorry I yelled. I know you want to bring down the Order, but we can't do it alone. We'll just be killed."

Twinkaleni sniffs, "But that's precisely what we're training for."

"We'll get there. It's just gonna take time," Alice assures the upset Murin.

"But we don't *have* time. We must strike while the war drains them."

"The war's been goin' on for years. I think it'll hold for a while longer."

Danahlia, chewing, has joined them and caresses one of Twinkaleni's large ears with a hand, her other still wrapped around the drumstick. The Murin is coaxed back to their packs and the trio settles down to eat.

During and after, the girls talk of their training, Twinkaleni outlining schedules and plans in some length while the others nod along with only a passing interest. Eventually, even the Murin tires and they all drift off to sleep.

Chapter 2

Barley Town

The next morning as the girls are walking, they hear a panicked commotion coming from somewhere ahead. Danahlia throws on the cloak of the Order to hide herself and the trio races up a wide hill to see what's causing it. In the shallow valley below, they spot three Lagomorphs atop a small wagon trying to fend off what look like large boars of some kind. The rabbit people are clearly in a bind, the largest of them jabbing and waving a hoe at the beasts encircling them and their frightened donkey, while shouting at her smaller kin to stay atop the wagon.

"What are those things?" asks Alice, watching a few of the boars that have broken off from the attack to surround something in the tall grass.

"Those're shatterheads! Twinkie, gimme the ring, hurry," Danahlia orders, holding her hand out to the mouse girl. Twinkaleni feels around in a pocket before handing the Liguna the enchanted ring retrieved from the defeated agent of the Order. Dropping her pack as she accepts it, Danahlia charges down the hill toward the besieged wagon, spear in hand.

Alice follows suit, taking a moment more to let her backpack and other gear slip off her shoulders while keeping her bow, a handful of arrows, and her sword. Twinkaleni hurries to catch up as well, nearly tripping over Alice's dropped supplies.

"What're shatterheads?" the Tokala asks, keeping pace with the Liguna.

Danalia raises her ringed hand at the group of boars nuzzling around in the grass, "They have hard boney foreheads they like to ram things with. You see one chargin', get outta the way. Adarath!"

A large ball of flame appears before her fingers and flies straight into the boars with a loud whoosh of hot parting air. The ball bursts as it hits the ground amidst the beasts sending them singed and squealing in all directions.

Alice jams her arrows into the ground and kneels behind them. Nocking one, she draws and takes aim at a boar grunting menacingly at the Lagomorphs. She lets loose, watching as it hits the large creature just below its shoulder making it squeal and run off only to tackle another to the ground in it's haste. Alice lets fly all her arrows, making several hits that cause the wounded to panic the others while Danahlia rushes in. The Liguna leaps atop the wagon screaming and stabbing anything that comes near, her intention not to kill but scatter the beasts. Twinkaleni lets loose with several bursts of fire on her approach, discouraging any of the frightened ferals from rallying.

Dropping the bow and running to join her friend on the wagon, Alice spots one of the boars Danahlia managed to scare with her fireball. It seems aware of the Liguna's part in the seared flesh on its flank, its eyes locking onto her as she harries others away from the rabbit people. Alice sees the boar stamp at the ground a few times with a fore hoof and she dashes ahead of it with sword drawn, suspecting what is to come next. The boar lets out an angry grunt and charges right for Danahlia the moment she jumps off the wagon to scare off another boar harassing the bound donkey.

Alice runs as fast as she can to intercept the furious beast and just as she comes along side it, she slashes at the hog's rear leg, taking the hoof clean off. The creature squeals in pain tumbling and rolling with its own momentum. Hearing this Danahlia turns as the boar slides before her, kicking up dirt as it flails. Without hesitation, the Liguna thrusts her crab leg tipped spear deep into its chest before moving on to others.

Twinkaleni slowly descends the hill, firing streams of flame at the retreating beasts, carefully angling her shots over the grass as not to catch it. Two other boars were too injured to run off and Danahlia finishes one, leaving the last to Alice. The young fox girl tries not to think about the life she is ending as she slashes its throat, keeping a safe distance so as to avoid the last of its wild trashing.

The threat ended, the girls converge on the wagon and the three Lagomorphs. The largest, a woman of tan fur and blue eyes, thanks them profusely while getting the smaller two down from the bed of the wagon. She then tries to calm the donkey, which is crying out in distress but at least doesn't appear injured. Danahlia tosses some dirt over the fire that's started from her fireball as Alice approaches the rabbit folk.

"Are you all right?" she asks, sheathing her sword.

Thankfully, the only thing damaged was the cargo of carrots she and her two small children were transporting. The Lagomorph mother introduces herself as Lulu, a local carrot farmer on her way to trade in a town called Barley.

"Your magic," Lulu says to Twinkaleni, "And your cloak," she says looking to Danahlia, "Are you from the Order of Thermathrogi? Have you come to tell me of my Lemmy? How is he? Is he well?"

Alice and Twinkaleni share a look as Danahlia walks over, "Who?"

"Lemmy, a boy about this height, with large blue eyes, and fur of this color," Lulu says in a flurry of gestures ending with her tugging down one of her long ears. She then points accusingly at Danahlia, "You lot took him away to that school seven months ago to be raised as a mage."

"He's our big brother. Have you brought him back? Where is he?" the little Lagomorph girl asks, holding onto an even smaller sibling.

"We've been on the road for some time now and have heard nothing of your Lemmy," says Twinkaleni.

The rabbit woman's shoulders slump, her gaze falling as she gives a defeated, "Oh… well, thank you again for your help."

Twinkaleni clenches her jaw before offering, "I'm sure the Order is taking very good care of him. Those with the touch of magic are greatly valued, especially in these troubled times."

From what the Murin has told her of life in the Order, Alice knows this to be a great lie but it seems to comfort the young mother some.

"Yes, they say he will become a great mage one day. Are you a mage? Are the conditions in the Order agreeable? Are you fed well?" the rabbit woman asks Twinkaleni, clearly desperate for news of her son.

"I am still in training, and yes, quite agreeable," replies Twinkaleni leaning away as Lulu gets closer to her.

The woman smiles, scrunching up her plain brown skirt and nearly coming to tears, "That is good to hear. And you yourself are so young. The ones who took Lemmy said it would be a great many years before he had mastered his gifts. Does this mean he'll be allowed to see us soon?"

Twinkaleni looks to her companions uncertainly, "Um, I, suppose it is possible-"

"When?" asks Lulu, "Is there a certain age or will he be allowed to leave on his own or-?"

Alice interrupts, "It depends, on his abilities and, uh, how fast he can, master them."

"Yes, yes," Twinkaleni nods, "I mastered basic evocation rather quickly and so was given leave, under the guidance of my master," she indicates Danahlia, who wears the red cloak embroidered with the golden eye in a triangle, the symbol of the order, "to gain more practical field experience."

The once shredded cloak the girls had salvaged from the now dead mage hunter the Order sent after Twinkaleni had been repaired by one of the widows the girls had stayed with. The color of the patches is a bit off but in dim light, and from a distance, one could hardly tell.

"Oh, I see. And your master is a Liguna?" the woman asks, looking to Danahlia.

"I am," Danahlia answers sternly, keeping her hood up and face turned away from the Lagomorphs.

"Indeed. The Order is pressed for resources and trusts my master to this task," says Twinkaleni hurriedly.

"Oh, I'm sorry, I didn't mean to offend. It's just, been a long while since I've seen one... of your kind I mean."

"Make's sense considering the war," puts in Alice.

The mother forces a smile, "Y-yes, I suppose it does."

The bit of tension that's built up defuses as more questions and answers are exchanged. Lulu checks on the woven basket of carrots the boars had managed to knock off her wagon but finds most have been devoured and those left were burnt. She has several more full baskets and makes it known she still intends to go to Barley. The girls gather their things and wonder what to do with the three defeated shatterheads. They can't carry any more supplies and the boars might weigh a hundred pounds each at least. Danahlia can't be convinced to leave so much meat behind so Lulu offers them the use of her wagon to take the wild hogs into town where they can be properly butchered and sold.

In agreement, Alice and Danahlia load the wagon with the fallen beasts but the extra weight proves too much for the exhausted donkey to handle with passengers. This means they have to walk, and sometimes push, their way toward the settlement. Lulu explains that she tried to take a less traveled path to avoid the rumors of bandits on the main roads but ended up encountering the shatterheads instead. The donkey tried to get them to safety but wore itself out pulling the wagon through the grass.

"Bandits?" asks Danahlia from behind the wagon.

"Oh yes, bandits are all over I hear. With so few patrols protecting the roads, they've become bold over the last few years. We haven't seen any, gods be praised, but there are a lot of grievances about them," reveals Lulu.

Twinkaleni tugs on Alice's blouse and the girls gather behind the wagon to talk in private.

"Are you both quite sure you want to go to this town? It may be dangerous," whispers Twinkaleni.

"But what about the meat money?" Danahlia whispers back, "Plus, shatterheads are good eatin', we should try to take some with us."

"Yeah, and Lulu already believes we're part o' the Order. If we can convince the town's people too, maybe we won't have to keep hidin' all the time," adds Alice.

"That'd be nice," agrees Danahlia.

"You two want to take such a risk for some pig meat and a maybe?" asks Twinkaleni, clearly finding their reasoning questionable.

Danahlia and Alice share a look then nod to the Murin, who sighs.

"By the way, if you're training her," Lulu wonders, pointing to Danahlia and then Twinkaleni, "What does that make you?" she finishes, directing the question to Alice.

"Uh, I, am, their... guard," blurts Alice.

"Yup, our faithful protector, young but skilled as you yourself saw," adds Danahlia confidently.

Lulu raises her chin in a slow nod of uncertain comprehension and Danahlia turns back to Twinkaleni, whispering, "See? We got this."

As they walk on, Lulu asks a great many questions about the Order and life there while telling the girls a little about herself. She reveals the agents who took her son had told her very little about it, only that he would become an individual of great importance to the kingdom. Lulu's husband was off at war, leaving her to watch over the children and the carrots they grew. Lemmy, the eldest of her three children, was sorely needed on the farm but when the Order came, there was no denying them. Lulu now struggles to raise her young children and work the fields, but with the help of neighbors she had still managed to cultivate a decent crop this season. She borrowed the donkey and wagon in the hopes that she would be able to sell and trade her carrots for enough to get them through the coming winter. The loss of one of her precious baskets clearly troubles her but she makes praises to the gods that it hadn't been any worse.

Alice finds it uncomfortable to hear about gods. Once upon a time, she had dutifully praised and prayed to the ones she knew but after the loss of both her parents to the war, the young fox had rather lost interest in the seemingly negligent beings. Alice preferred to rely on herself to produce results and let the gods and goddesses leave her out of their machinations. Still, she never said anything to others about this, knowing how devout and even fanatical people could be about their beliefs.

The town is not terribly far from where the wagon was attacked and by late evening they make it into the outskirts. Barley turns out to be quite large. As they venture further in, the houses and shops get crammed closer and closer together until there are no fields, yards, or gardens, only roads and buildings. People of all descriptions hustle about in the waning sunlight and the girls, particularly Danahlia, draw no small number of looks.

Many of the more carnivorous residents also seem keenly interested in the three hogs hanging limply from the small, donkey drawn wagon. Some of these even begin to follow along, calling offers for various cuts of meat. Lulu tells the girls that they are likely to get the fairest price at an inn she knows called the Bear's Den.

On their way there, a Houdain, missing much of his right arm, shouts, "What the far flung crap is a Cold Blood doin' here?!"

The dog man looks haggard and dirty, Alice also notices he is missing an ear. Two others flank him, looking just as distastefully at the lizard girl.

"Idiot, she's with that order for magic folk," calls one of those following the wagon, a Feladine woman.

"Says some red cloth with a bit o' gold thread!" the Houdain snarls back, eyes never leaving Danahlia as he approaches, "I say she's one o' the smoothies sneakin' there way 'round these parts." The two who flank him growl their agreement.

Lulu ignores this but tries to coax her donkey into moving faster while Danahlia pulls her hood up a bit more to hide her face.

"We *are* of the Order of Thermathrogi," claims Alice, trying to force a confidence she doesn't feel.

"Says who?!" the Houdain barks back, getting within arm's reach of the trio.

Alice jumps at the harshly spat words, but Danahlia turns to him angrily, "Says this. Adarath!"

As the enchanted ring glows a furious red, Danahlia throws her hand out to the Houdain, only to raise it up just before a fireball flies free from it and into the darkening sky. Cries of alarm go up from those nearest and the dog man falls back into his companions, taking them all to the ground.

"The Order does not care for impediments. Consider this your only warning," Danahlia spits venomously, glaring down at the fallen men.

As they move on, chatter arises and word spreads of what transpired. Alice looks around to find even more people are following now, though at a safe distance.

"That was either brave or foolish," comments Twinkaleni.

"Don't forget fun," Danahlia grins, "And now people know not to mess with us."

"They also know we have an enchanted ring and the word to activate it," the Murin tosses back.

"So? Who's gonna try to take it from someone who can hurl fireballs in their faces?" the Liguna argues.

Twinkaleni sighs, "Enchanted items are extremely rare and, as you so publicly demonstrated, powerful."

"Oh," nods Alice, seeing where the mouse mage is leading them.

"What?" asks Danahlia.

"They're worth a lot," answers Alice.

"Indeed," Twinkaleni grumbles, "So as to whom, I believe *thieves* would have a passing interest in valuable, rare, and powerful items, don't you?"

"Psh, you're over thinkin' it, we'll be alright," assures Danahlia with a negligent wave of her ringed hand.

It's nearly dark out when the wagon finally comes to a stop before a large, wooden, two-story building. Light and the sounds of a merry crowd pour from a great open door, above which is a worn sigh dangling from rusted chains. The sign depicts two smiling bears in profile, clinging mugs together before the mouth of a cave. Under it reads, "Bear's Den."

"Well, here we are," announces Lulu.

The Lagormorph mother lowers her daughter and son from where they helped guide the donkey atop the wagon as the girls gather there things and prepare to enter the inn. The small crowd that's gathered behind them begins to converge, intending to follow, when Danahlia suddenly turns to them with a swish of her cloak.

The nearest to her start in surprise as she pans a clawed finger over them, saying, "Don't touch our pigs."

The doorway opens into an expansive well lit room with a diverse dozen or so patrons. Around several assorted tables they eat, drink, and a few even sing. Alice follows Lulu and her children in, with Twinkaleni and Danahlia trailing behind. A plump, black furred Urock in a simple, pale green dress and well used apron pours something from a pitcher into the mugs of three men at a table. Her patrons cheer her on and slap a few brins on the table for her service.

As she gathers them, the large bear woman notices the new arrivals and calls, "Lulu! We hear you coming soon. Sit, sit, I get you something." She speaks with an unfamiliar accent in a deep voice as she gestures to an empty table.

The Urock then lumbers to the back of the room and shouts into a doorway there, "Artyom! Guess who just come in." Alice can only hear what sounds like a low rumbling roar in return but the woman replies, "Is Lulu, and she brought the little ones. Get them something warm, eh."

Alice and her friends take seats at their own table near Lulu and her children. They watch as many of those who followed them do the same. A Lobovan woman who had already made a few offers for pieces of their shatterheads does so again, wanting a few legs for five brins each.

Before the girls can make any reply, the Urock woman roars, "You! What is Cold Blood doing here?!"

The other patrons go quiet as the Urock woman closes on Danahlia with surprising speed, knocking over an empty chair with her girth.

The Lobovan hurriedly backs away but Lulu stand up and shouts, "Its ok, Misha! They're with the Order of Thermathrogi."

The Urock woman stops to glare over Danahlia and her companions, letting out a breath through her nostrils, she then glances to Lulu, "The magic people?"

"Yes, they also saved me and my bunnies from a pack of shatterheads on the way here," says the Lagomorph mother, smiling at the girls.

Lulu's daughter, Lolo, bubbles, "Yeah! We saw them shoot fire and arrows and they have swords and got three of 'em!"

Misha looks down her nose at the girls and crosses her arms over her wide chest, "You save Lulu and little ones?"

Twinkaleni's eyes and mouth are wide open as she stares wordlessly at the large woman towering over them, so Danahlia answers, "Uh, yeah, I guess we did, didn't we?"

"Ye-yeah, yeah, we did. And we brought some of the shatterheads to... trade," Alice nods up at the imposing Misha.

Before the Urock can say anything, an even larger, brown one emerges from the back room. He has to stoop, turn to the side, and suck in his gut, to get through the doorway but once in the main hall he puts on a big grin and hobbles over, a few bowls of something steaming in his massive hands. Alice notices the strange way he walks and looks to his rather short stumpy legs to find an actual wooden stump has replaces one at about mid-thigh.

As he walks, his stump thumps the wood of the floor heavily and he calls, "Lulu!" in a deep but friendly baritone, accented the same as Misha, "We not see you in long while."

"Artyom," greets Lulu, walking up to meet the bear man and give him a hug. The rabbit woman looks small and fragile before the furry giant who needs to bend at the waist just to loosely wrap an arm around her.

"Ah, and children too. Little Lolo, looking more beautiful every day, just like mama. And who dis? Can't be Levi. So big now!" Artyom says to the small rabbit children, "Going to be great warrior like papa, ha?" The tiny Lagomorph boy flexes his arms with a toothy smile and the gigantic Urock laughs heartily, "Ha! You be stronger than Artyom one day." Then he notices Misha still standing over Alice's little group, "Eh? What is dis? A Liguna? Here?"

"They're with me," Lulu is quick to say as the massive man sets down the bowls on Lulu's table before turning to Danahlia, one fuzzy brow raised.

"Lulu say they save her from shatterheads," informs Misha, and then adds distastefully, "with magic."

"Mages of the Order, eh?" Artyom grumbles, not so much a question but a comment, as a large hand comes up to stroke his chin.

Twinkaleni's eyes and mouth have somehow gotten wider, the great Urock seeming to loom over her despite being several feet away.

Even Danahlia is having trouble coming up with a response, but then Alice points at the Murin, "Um, she's the mage," then to Danahlia, "she's her, uh, master," and then to herself, "and I'm, I'm a um..." Alice's mind goes blank as she looks into the massive man's questioning, brown eyes.

"A guard," provides Lulu.

"That so?" the Urock man asks, looking them over.

The girls nod.

Artyom frowns, looking down at them, then his cheeks puff out, unable to keep a straight face, "Buha! Well, if you friends with Lulu, then you welcome here." He then claps his hands together, snapping the girls out of their daze, "Heh heh, Misha, we must get these people fed, come."

Misha gives the girls a smile before the two Urocks make their way to the back room. At the doorway, Misha picks up a little chef's hat that must have fallen off Artyom's head, because she reaches up to place it over one of his round ears.

Alice lets out a pent up breath as Twinkaleni says in awe, "I had no idea people could get so, so...."

"Yeah, that *is* a big'un," comments Danahlia.

Lulu leans over to them, "No worries girls, he's as sweet as they come."

"Thanks for steppin' in for us," says Alice, sincerely.

The Lagomorph woman smiles as she slides bowls before her children and they start to eat what looks like vegetable soup. After a few minutes, the

Urocks return with more bowls for the girls and other patrons.

As Artyom passes them around he encourages, "Eat, eat, good food, help grow," putting a single thick finger on Twinkaleni's tiny shoulder.

Alice tries the soup, finding it *is* quite good. The stock is flavorful and the soup is hardy with thick cuts of potatoes, mushrooms, onions, and other vegetables that are soft but not mushy. The mountainous man smiles as the girls enjoy his soup before moving on to serve his other customers.

The trio eats, having gotten rather hungry after the day's travel. While they do, one of the men from before, a Tokala like Alice though, his fur is darker with brown undertones, begins to sing again in a pleasant cheery tone.

Sooo I Met a girl in ol' Barley town,
Sweetest thing that could be foun'
Pretty, kind and awfully fine,
I told her one day she'd be mine.

Went really well for at least a while,
Then war broke out in the western isle.
Man rode in to tell us all,

That it was time ta' answer war's ol' call.

Met a girl in ol' Barley town,
Sweetest thing that could be foun'
Pretty, kind and awfully fine,
I told her one day she'd be mine.

(As a few people begin to clap and bang mugs against their tables to his song, he stands up looking to a female Lutarin sitting beside him. The otter woman looks shyly away as he takes her hand to kiss the back of it.)

Kissed her hand, bein' sent away,
Told her that I'd be back one day.
Went afar, a blade in hand,
(He swings an imaginary sword for emphasis)
Fought all over a foreign land.

Thought of her near all the time,
Thinkin' of when that she'd be mine.
Wonderin' if she'd wait for me,
After this dang war I'd see.

Guys askin' what I'm thinkin' of,
I tell 'em it's this girl I love.
They want me to elaborate,
So listen good and I'll tell ya mate,

(By now Alice and most of the other patrons are clapping along.)

I met a girl in ol' Barley town,
Sweetest thing that could be foun'
Pretty, kind and awfully fine,
I told her one day she'd be mine.

Fightin' hard until the day,
I lost a hand while in the fray.
        (The Tokala holds up his left arm, which ends in a stump at the wrist)
Got sent home, it had been a while,
Since I went off to the western isle.

Found the girl I said be mine,
Still pretty, kind, and awfully fine,
Waited all this time for me,
And now together we two be.

He ends with an affectionate kiss on the woman's lips, that's returned and then some to the sounds of cheering and clapping. Alice claps enthusiastically too, finding it a beautiful display. And as more drinks are poured and bellies are filled, more songs are sung and a few stories heard. The girls keep to themselves for the most part, though are still badgered by offers for their meat. Lulu has taken Artyom's ear, and he sits in two chairs, that even then seem to struggle to hold his bulk, while they talk.

A Lotarin girl hesitantly approaches Alice. She asks if she's the one who slew the shatterheads outside. Alice apologizes and tells the girl, who looks about her age, that they're planning to sell the pigs to Artyom. The Lotarin shakes her head, saying she wasn't asking about meat but says she's the daughter of cabbage farmers in the suburbs and one of many who have been having trouble with the growing number of shatterheads. Apparently, the wild ferals like cabbages just as much as carrots and have been ravaging her family's crop fields. She was sent into town to seek help.

Alice leans into the center of her table to discuss the matter with her friends.

"Sounds great. We save the farms and get more pigs to eat and sell," says Danahlia.

Twinkaleni needs to stand on her chair with tiny hands on the table to join the discussion, "We should think this through before agreeing to anything. Even if we hunt these creatures, how are we to get them back to town? We had Lulu's wagon today."

Danahlia leans over to the Lagomorph mother, still talking with the massive Urock, "Hey Lulu, can we borrow your wagon to hunt some more shatterheads tomorrow?"

"Oh, I suppose so. I'll need to stay in town until I can sell my carrots, so I guess I won't *need* it," she replies uneasily.

"There, problem solved," the Liguna assures her companions.

Twinkaleni shakes her head in disappointment, "Don't you remember anything? She herself is borrowing the wagon. What if it's damaged or we lose the donkey?"

Alice lowers her bowl after a sip, "We'll watch it."

Danahlia nods, "Yeah, you worry too much, pint size."

Twinkaleni narrows her eyes at the Liguna and Alice adds, "If we get enough for the shatterheads, maybe we can even rent our own wagon or somethin'."

Danahlia points to her with a spoon, mouth full of soup, "Mh-hm," she chews and swallows, "You see how much these people want the meat. I bet we could make a lot."

"You plan to hunt shatterheads?" wonders Artyom, taking interest in their conversation.

"Uh, yeah. We already got a few, brought them here because Lulu said you might want to buy them," informs Alice.

"You bring here? Why not say something? Come, show me," the massive man replies, rising, his wooden chairs creaking in relief.

He leads the girls, Lulu, the raccoon girl, and a few others out to the wagon, still parked just outside. The donkey makes a distressed noise at his approach and Lulu moves to calm it.

"Oh," the Urock says with mirth, "Three. You girls are good hunters." He then reaches in to wrap one hand around the largest of the hogs' throats and lifts it out of the wagon with evident ease. He bobs it in the air and laughs, "Ha! Good weight too. I take all, seven shil each."

Alice turns to her friends excitedly, "What do you think?" The Murin and Liguna nod their approval and Alice turns to the massive man, holding out a hand, "Deal."

They shake, Alice's hand only able to grasp three of Artyom's thick fingers. He then gathers the other boars, carrying them all close to his chest in a bear hug, "Good, good. You stay here tonight. I make good stew with this for breakfast, ha!"

Everyone heads back in, those interested in meat now following Artyom around. The Lotarin asks if Alice and her friends will help with the shatterheads and the girls agree to follow her to her farm tomorrow to see about it. The young girl thanks them gratefully before wandering off into the night. Back at their table, the girls finish supper and Misha comes by, beckoning them to follow her upstairs to their room for the night.

The stairs lead to a hall with several doors on one side and a few candles hanging from the wall on the other. Some of the doors are open as guests still wander the hall and settle in. The one Misha leads the girls to is closed. The moment the Urock opens the door and they get a look in, Twinkaleni calls dibs on one of the two beds, running up and tossing her backpack on it. She had gotten very good at doing so while the girls traveled through the country, where most of the places they stayed had only so much room to offer. Misha smiles placing a small purse heavy with coin, a lit candle, and the room key on a round table by the door. She wishes them a goodnight before departing, closing the door after her.

The room is cozy, well-kept and clean, if sparsely furnished. There is no window and only the one door, the two beds against opposite walls. The small table has a twin beside the bed opposite the one Twinkaleni has chosen, but the one by the door has a single chair accompanying it. The table beside the bed has a large wash bowl filled with water and a few small towels. The girls make use of these to clean themselves a bit as they discuss their future.

Alice locks and unlocks the door a few times, not having used a key since living in her old house in Toki village, "Seven shils per shatterhead. We could get rich if we can hunt enough."

"Yeah," moans Danahlia, stretching out under the sheet of her bed after having counted twenty one shils in the purse, "Can't wait for you guys to try 'em in that stew."

"So you wanna stay here for a little bit? Hunting those ferals could be good training," Alice says, looking over to Twinkaleni but the Murin is already sound asleep.

Alice smiles, locks the door, and leaves the key on the table nearest it. She picks up the candle but then considers for a moment which bed to take, Danahlia in one and Twinkaleni in the other. The Liguna holds open the sheet for her and Alice grins, placing the candle on the table near them to lie beside her cold blooded friend.

Chapter 3

The Bear's Den

This wasn't the first time Alice had shared a bed with Danahlia and if she were to be honest, she preferred it to sleeping alone. Though she never said so. Both their heads rest on either side of the single pillow as they adjust, getting comfortable. Alice's leg runs over Danahlia's, her toes brushing the smooth skin of the lizard girl's calf. She's about to apologize when their eyes meet. She pauses. She had seen the Liguna's eyes a hundred times before of course, but something is different about them tonight. It's subtle, perhaps just the dimness of the room or even the flickering candle light itself, Alice isn't sure, but something is new. She looks deeper, curious, and for some reason a little afraid.

Danahlia's eyes are green, as they had always been, but so very green. Looking closer, Alice finds they seem to be filled with sand, each grain a jewel glowing in a slightly different hue from all the others. The colors twinkle and dance in the sporadic light and Alice feels her lips parting as she wanders over the dazzling array, marveling at how one color could have so many shades. They all seem to pull her toward Danahlia's vertical pupil, like a bottomless canyon just opening in the middle of a glittering desert. She tries to see deeper into it, wondering how many other beautiful greens might have fallen down there when their noses touch.

They jerk away from each other, Danahlia mumbling, "Ah, hey."

Alice feels her fur bristle and body tense with embarrassment as she blurts, "Uh, sorry."

"What were you lookin' at?" asks Danahlia, a clawed hand coming up to rub the tip of her muzzle.

Alice rolls to look at the ceiling, suddenly feeling very self-conscious, "Buh, nothin', nothin'."

Danahlia purses her lips, "Well, you were lookin' at it pretty hard. Why's your nose wet?"

"I don't know, it just is. It's always like that."

"Huh."

After a few moments of stiff staring at the wood plank ceiling, Alice feels a growing sense of unease and looks over to see Danahlia watching her.

The fox girl raises a brow, "What are *you* lookin' at?"

Danahlia grins, still staring, "Nothin'."

Alice rolls back to return her stare, a little flustered. Their toes mingle a bit under the sheet and after only a few seconds of watching Danahlia's grin, Alice can't help but smile too.

The smile turns into a little laugh and Danahlia asks, "What?" unable to keep from laughing herself.

"Nothin'," Alice returns, laughing for no apparent reason, an unfamiliar but pleasant little warmth bubbling inside of her. From under the sheet, one of Danahlia's hands rises up to stroke Alice's cheek. It's a slow, gentle touch that reminds her of when they first met. Even so it makes Alice freeze with uncertainty.

Danahlia seems amused by the reaction, letting her fingers push back a little fur, "You're really pretty." They both freeze then as Danahlia catches herself, her gaze falling to focus intently on Alice's chin, hand pulling away, "Uh, I mean, for a, fuzzy tailed, fur faced, uh, pointy eared…"

While Danahlia stammers, a torrent of questions floods through Alice's mind. *What's going on? What happened? Did something change? What do I do? She thinks I'm pretty? What does that mean? Does she like me? Does she like like me? Do I like her? Should I like her? Can I like her? What changed? I'm pretty? Does it mean anything? What do I say? Do I say thank you? Would that sound stupid? Should I say anything? What should I do?*

Seconds become an eternity that spans only a minute as she watches Danahlia look down and away from her. Seeing the confusion, and perhaps a little hurt, on her friend's face, Alice forces the sea of questions aside to reveal one single answer hidden at the bottom. *I do like her.*

After a deep breathe, Alice gathers her courage and leans in, giving Danahlia the smallest lick on the tip of her nose before immediately pulling back. Danahlia looks at her, beautiful emerald eyes widening as if she's seeing something truly astonishing or perhaps immensely frightening. Her own embarrassment, fear, and uncertainty leave Alice unable to wait even a second for a response. She rolls away and looks at Twinkaleni, slumbering peacefully only a few feet away in the other bed. But then she considers and scoots back a little until she can just feel Danahlia's body against her tail.

In her mind, rapid calculations are made as she tells herself, *Ok, you made your move. You could not have been more clear, now wait and see what she does. Oh ticks, was it clear? What if she thought it was gross? Why isn't she doing anything?! You licked her, that's, affectionate... right? Maybe you should just sleep on the floor. Oh ticks, you licked her. Do Liguna even do that? What is wrong with you!? Where did you even get that? That was so stupid! You made things weird. You should sleep on the floor.*

Alice is seriously contemplating just rolling off the bed when she feels Danahlia's hand glide over her arm, and then a leg over her thigh. The lizard girl pulls her in lightly while pressing her warm, soft body against the fox girl's back. Alice then feels Danahlia's chin come to rest atop her head between her ears and they flick a bit at the touch. Unsure as to what to do now, Alice stays as still as she can, not wanting to ruin anything. Danahlia settles, letting out a pleased little moan as she nuzzles the fur atop Alice's head, an arm wrapping about her stomach and a leg laying over her own. The fox girl finally exhales and relaxes, feeling very proud of herself and wonderfully comfortable in the Liguna's embrace.

That night she is fleeing through a forest, alone and scared. It's too dark and dense to see anything but the foliage before her as she pushes through, a terrible force stalking her. Without ever laying eyes on them, she knows the ghastly shades of the Rotan deserter and the Mustaroni agent are after her, made immortal by death and tireless with vengeance. She runs as fast as she can, plants wet and cold with dew whipping her as she flies past them. She nearly runs into the trunk of a great oak and veers off to the left. Running in this new direction she hears vague but somehow familiar voices telling her to keep going, that she's almost there.

"Over here," and "This way," they say from somewhere ahead, until she stumbles before a cave. It's too dark to see in it, but the voices call to her from inside, "It's safe in here, we're all safe here," another voice calls, "Hurry, before they find you."

Alice dashes inside, concealing herself in the shadows far from the cave's mouth. She sits with her back against the side, hoping the restless shades will pass her by when she notices a strange rock sticking out just on the edge of visible light. But it isn't a rock. It's a small hand. Then she comes to see she's surrounded by the charred corpses of the forest children, their bodies strewn about in heaps in the darkness, reeking of death and burnt meat. "You came back. Stay with us. It's safe here," the haunting little voices say from the dark still forms.

Alice is about to scream when she hears the foot falls of the two vengeful shades just outside. She clamps her hands around her muzzle, desperate to keep from making any noise as the sound of footsteps get louder. The small hand begins to move, stiff with rigamortis, and it's too much. Alice jolts awake, knocking Danahlia in the chin hard enough to make the larger girl's teeth clack together.

Danahlia grumbles, "Ugh, wha? What's wrong?"

Taking shallow rapid breaths, Alice looks around to find she's still in the room at the Bear's Den. The candle on the table beside her is still lit and hadn't even burned down that much. Twinkaleni is still slumbering peacefully in her own bed.

"Ticks, you're shakin," says Danahlia, wrapping herself a little more about the terrified Tokala.

Alice whispers, "It was, just a nightmare," as much to assure herself as the Liguna. She curls up a little more and lets herself be held.

It was infrequent that at least one of the girls wasn't taken from sleep by the specters of their past. If awoken by another, they would do their best to guard their frightened companion from such hauntings. Tonight it was Danahlia's turn to comfort Alice and the Liguna strokes the fox girl's arm, asking what it was about. Talking it out helped sometimes. It let them see just how preposterous some of the scenarios the subconscious concocted were, but other times, doing so only made them more real.

"I was-" Alice starts but then listens, the footsteps of her mind still echoing in her ears.

"You where what?" Danahlia wonders, her lower jaw brushing over Alice's head.

"Shh, listen."

The sound is coming from outside their room in the dimly lit hall.

"Probably just someone who needed to take a dump," suggests Danahlia, relaxing.

Alice continues to listen intently, the steps just outside their room. She watches the shadows of feet, barely visible in the sliver of candle light beneath the door. They stop.

"Danny," Alice whispers, nudging the Lizard girl with an elbow.

Danahlia takes in a breath and lifts her head to look, "Probably just forgot which room was-" After a little rustle, a subtle clicking can be heard from the door knob, different from the sounds the key would make.

"They're pickin' the lock," Alice whispers in alarm.

"Get your sword," Danahlia orders in a hushed tone, rising to retrieve her spear from where it leans against the wall at the foot of the bed.

Alice reaches for her scabbard under the bed and draws her weapon as silently as she can. She can see the blade is still stained with shatterhead blood. Ignoring this for now, she considers waking

Twinkaleni but Danahlia waves her urgently over to the door where the Liguna crouches with her spear.

Alice joins her, whispering in her ear, "Should we say something? Maybe they'll go away if they know we're awake."

Danahlia shakes her head and makes a bursting gesture with one hand. Alice takes this to mean she wants to surprise them. The Liguna then makes a few more gestures that Alice thinks means she intends to strike when the door opens and Alice is to back her. The fox girl nods and they both prepare to attack.

The lock ticks a few more times as the picker feels around for tumblers before it clicks. Alice is having trouble hearing it, her heart beats so loudly and she desperately tries to keep calm, sword shaking in her grip. The door knob begins to turn, slowly, carefully, and she can just hear the bolt sliding from the frame. Danahlia looks to her, putting a finger to her lips as she readies a thrust around waist height. Alice clenches her jaw, gripping her weapon even tighter. The door creaks open.

The moment there's a wide enough gap, Danahlia thrusts with her entire body, shouting, "Argh!"

Alice hears a surprised gasp just as the door swings open from the act, revealing two people in the hall. One, the lock picker, took Danahlia's spear high in the chest. It's the haggard Houdain from the walk to the inn, the one that Danahlia knocked into his companions with a fireball. He's on one knee looking in shock at the crab leg spear point embedded deep within him.

Once the other man, another Houdain, realizes what's happened, he lunges for Danahlia, a thick dagger in his hand, snarling, "You filthy little-"

With a shout of her own, Alice turns what was going to be a thrust into an upward slice that catches the man's dagger wielding hand, cutting it open with a light spray of warm blood. Unable to build much momentum, the wound isn't terribly deep but the dagger is sent flying away to bang loudly against the wall and floor. The man screams in pain, holding his wounded hand as Danahalia pulls free her spear from the first, the impaled Houdain slumping to the floor. Unarmed, alone, and facing two foes, the dog man loses what courage he had and runs down the hall to the stairs.

"What's happening?!" Twinkaleni squeaks from behind, making both girls jump.

"Nothin', we took care of it," assures Danahlia, letting out a breath.

A few of the other doors open and heads poke out to see what's going on, Lulu among them. The man Danahlia stabbed isn't dead, but doesn't seem interested in moving, a pool of blood steadily widening from under his crumpled form. Alice steadies her breathing, looking down at the dying man.

Down stairs they hear Artyom ask, "Who you?"

Then Misha's voice, "He didn't pay for room."

Alice shouts down the hall, "He's a thief! They tried to rob us!"

"Thief?!" Artyom growls, "In MY HOUAAAARGH!!" The last word turns into a bestial roar that echoes up the stairs and seems to shake the floorboards. Just under it Alice hears a loud thud. A few moments later, Artyom and Misha come up the stairs, the massive man wielding a stout club in one hand. "Another one?" Artyom asks, spotting the downed man.

"That's the man from before, the one you frightened with the fireball," illuminates Twinkaleni.

"Yeah, he's on his way out though," confirms Danahlia.

The downed Houdain glares at the Liguna, "You filthy, bug suckin', bareback, puddle hoppin', egg ploppin', rock huggin'-"

"Oh shut up and die already," snarls Danahlia, rising to her feet.

"Girls ok? Anyone hurt?" asks Misha, holding up a candle behind Artyom, unable to pass him in the hall.

"We're fine," Alice assures shakily.

"You get him good, huh?" asks the Urock man, approaching the Houdain. He then crouches down to hold the club before the dog man's eyes, baring his teeth, "I get you friend good, too." Artyom then nearly lifts the man by one arm, looking to his startled guests, "I so sorry. Everyone, please, back to beds." Then to the girls he says, "I take care of dis."

He turns then, dragging the man toward the stairs. Misha ducks into another room so he can pass, then shakes her head at the blood trailing on her once clean floor. She avoids stepping on it as she heads to the girl's room.

The trio makes way for her and to the other guests she waves, "Thieves all gone. Please, back to sleep, no charge tonight." She skips over the pool of blood before their door with surprising grace and then looks over the three girls, "You sure ok? No one hurt?"

"No, we're fine thanks," assures Alice again.

"We got them before they got us," adds Danahlia.

They sit on their bed to explain what happened. Twinkaleni is opposite them on her own bed and Misha sits beside her to hear their story. As the Urock does, the bed creaks and dips a bit, sending Twinkaleni sliding into the large woman's side. Misha picks her up and sets her in her lap, stroking the tiny girl's light gray fur as she listens. The mage endures this with an uncomfortable expression. When they finish and assure her again that they are unharmed, Misha offers to stay with them for the night. They gratefully refuse and she apologizes again, letting Twinkaleni go, commenting that most thieves tend to stay well away from the Bear's Den.

Alone again, the girls use the water in the wash bowl and towels to clean their weapons and each other. While Danahlia is wiping a damp cloth over some blood along Alice's neck, the fox girl wonders aloud as to why her sword didn't burn away the blood along its edge like it usually does.

"Enchanted items have finite amounts of energy within them," explains Twinkaleni, yawning and laying back down, "I'm rather surprised that Jellybane's power lasted this long. I suppose that is testament to the enchanting skill of the pixies."

"Is Jellybane a regular sword now?" Alice asks, a little disappointed.

"I suppose if more (yawn) energy were to be properly channeled into it by an adept enchanter, its powers could be restored," the sleepy Murin replies.

Looking over Alice's fur for any more blood stains, Danahlia says, "You need to hurry up and learn enchantin' so you can recharge our gear, Twinkie."

The Murin mage huffs in irritation, "Easier said than done, I assure you. It might be best not to have charges in such items," she then says pointedly, turning away from them, "No doubt it would make us less attractive to thieves."

As the girls try to settle back down, Alice finds herself wide awake, listening to Misha and Artyom cleaning the mess in the hall through the door. She can hear them talking in low voices as they scrub the floor. Their speech is muffled and in a language Alice doesn't understand but from their tones, Misha sounds irritated while Artyom seems apologetic. Knowing the two imposing bear people are just outside is rather comforting and after a while Alice blows out the candle to fall asleep.

The next morning, the girls wake to the wonderful aroma of warm food. Following their noses, they find the hall cleared of blood, only a vague stain left behind. Downstairs, they see several people already sitting at tables, bowls of delicious smelling stew before them. Lulu waves the girls over to her table where she sits with her children, eager to know of the goings on of the last night.

"You guys killed someone?" asks Lolo as they're discussing it.

"Nah, just poked him real good," says Danahlia.

Before they can continue, Misha arrives with bowls of stew for the girls. She tells them to go into the back room after they eat because Artyom wants to see them. The stew smells divine and they eagerly dig in. Misha smiles and tells them her husband makes the best shatterhead stew in town before moving on to other tables. Alice had never had shatterhead stew but it immediately becomes a favorite. The stew is thick with potatoes, garlic, carrots, and other earthy flavors, while the savory meat is so tender it practically falls apart in her mouth. The broth has absorbed the flavors of all the ingredients, turning it into a delightful medley that demands to be gobbled.

Alice and Danahlia are working on seconds, when the Lotarin from last night shows up and asks if they're ready to follow her to her farm. Then Lulu surprises them by saying she's going too.

"Nah, you don't need to go, it could be dangerous," warns Danahlia with a shake of her head.

"That wagon is my responsibility. Besides, do any of you know how to drive a donkey?" Lulu counters.

The girls don't and Alice asks, "What about your kids and sellin' your carrots?"

"Misha has agreed to look after them for me," replies Lulu, "So, are we ready?"

Unable to come up with any other reasons she shouldn't come, the girls ask the eager Lotarin to wait for a few more minutes as they go see what Artyom wanted.

The trio finds the door in the back of the main hall leads to a large kitchen, which has a few doorways that lead elsewhere. The massive Urock has his back to them as he drops some freshly cut chunks of meat into a large cauldron, one of three, set over a low fire in an impressive brick fireplace. He turns, wiping his hands on a heavily stained apron and spots Alice and her friends.

"Girls," he booms, "how you like stew?"

"Marvelous," says Twinkaleni.

"It was the best I ever had," says Alice truthfully.

"Great! We're definitely comin' back for dinner," chimes Danahlia wandering to the cauldron, "Ya makin' more?"

"Good good," the big man grins, "Oh yes, much more. Expect many people come for dis." He gives the stew a few stirs with a large, long handled spoon, "Bear's Den is famous for stew, you know? Have not had in while, people will be eager." He then takes a deep inhale, nodding satisfactorily, "Secret to good stew is long time over low heat. Maybe I teach you so you cook for your little ones, eh?" He chuckles to himself.

Misha comes in, swiftly making her way around the girls to one of the other cauldrons. She fills a few bowls with stew and two mugs with something from a barrel before hustling back out.

"I do hope word of the thieves from last night won't damage your business," says Twinkaleni.

"Maybe if they get away. But two thieves caught and no one hurt, very good. People say, 'Bear's Den is safe place,'" Artyom smiles at the tiny Murin, "You are mage, yes?"

"Mage in training," Twinkaleni replies with a nod.

"Hmm," Artyom says, his attention back to stirring, "In war, I see magic do many great things," he pauses a moment looking back at the smallest girl, "and many terrible things also. You train slow. Maybe war is over before it need you, eh?" He grins and then goes back to stirring his stew.

After a minute, the girls just standing about looking around the kitchen, Alice asks, "Misha said you wanted us for something?"

In the middle of examining a spoon full of stew, Artyom's brow rises, "Hmm? Oh, yes, of course. For hunting, come."

He leaves his spoon in the cauldron to lead the girls to one of the rooms even further back. This was apparently the Urocks' living quarters as it is well furnished with a gigantic bed, various other homie bits, and lit with early sunlight let in by several windows.

As the man hobbles along, he tells the girls, "Used to hunt all the time, now, Artyom too slow, boar always run away. You girls put shatterhead stew back on the menu, good for business. I lend you something, help hunt more."

Curious, Alice asks, "What happened to your leg?"

Artyom waves negligently to his wooden stump, "Eh, took arrow to knee," He turns and points to Danahlia, "Your people very good with bow," then he ponders for a moment, "Or maybe Artyom too big, easy target, ha!"

The wall the bear man walks up to has two thickly hafted spears set upon it, one crossed over the other. He takes one down and shows it to the girls, "This spear, made for hunting boar."

It was clearly forged by experienced hands, not cobbled together like Danahlia's weapon. Their thick hafts look heavy and sturdy while their steel, leaf-shaped blades are wide and flat. Just below the blades there are metal wings poking out on either side several inches long, though they don't look sharp.

Artyom pretend thrusts with the spear, "You get boar," he indicates the wings with a finger, "These keep boar from getting you back."

The girls nod their understanding and he hands the first to Danahlia, the second to Alice. Twinkaleni is far too small to handle one. Accepting the weighty spear, Alice wonders, "Does Misha go hunting with you?"

"Oh, no, that one for my son, Alexei," the Urock gives them a somber smile, "Maybe when war is over, we go hunting again." After a few seconds the massive man claps, "But for now, up to you. Bring me lots of boars hehha!"

Artyom leads the girls back into the kitchen where one of the shatterheads is in the process of being butchered on a long table in one corner. It's still fairly intact letting the Urock point out a small area just above and behind the forelimbs of the beast, "Heart and lungs here. You come in from side," he makes a thrusting gesture with a phantom spear, "thrust hard and low, make quick kill." He circles a finger over much of the beast's front shoulder, "Shatterhead have thick bone and cartilage here, tough to get through. Good way is one distract from front, other attack from side. I know you know how to kill, but this maybe help. I want many," Artyom grins and the girls thank him for the advice.

The trio meet back with Lulu along with the the Lotarin in the main hall and soon depart on their shatterhead hunting trip.

Now that the wagon is empty of carrots and beasts, the girls are allowed to ride in the back. Alice is especially grateful for this. After eating so much stew, she was *not* looking forward to having to walk anywhere. Lulu drives the small wagon west, following the worried Lotarin's directions. While the girl goes on about the problems the shatterheads are causing, she reminds Alice more and more of Ashleigh, her Didel friend back in Toki, Alice's hometown.

The two are different species but they're of a height and have somewhat similar coloring. Though what really makes Alice think of her friend is the Lotarin's speech. She has a more rural twang but little things like the inflections on some of her words and the sort of rushed way she talks, as if she wants to fill each breath with as many words as she can, makes her sound a lot like Ashleigh. Though it could just be how worried she clearly is.

Her name is Meeka and she seems to have developed the habit of stroking her thick, black ringed tail when agitated. Her fur is dominantly gray with white surrounding the black patches around her eyes and nose. As she talks, she keeps glancing forward as if already expecting to see her farm, "... and then they hit the Tuftpaw's spinach. It didn't take 'em long to eat up all their crop, the Tuftpaw's don't have much land, but from there they started in on the Swigtail's onions. After that, all the near folk come together to shoo 'em off, but those shatterheads fought back and some got hurt awful bad. So then my momma sends me inta town to look for anyone willin' to help, 'n' after seein' how you took down three of 'em yourselves, I thought you'd do just fine." Meeka looks down at her tail, still stroking it, "Oh, I, probly shouda told y'all, we don't really have any money or nothin'. Those pigs just 'bout ate all we had. Now with it bein' fall and all, folk are worried we ain't gonna have nothin' for winter time. It's just such a horrible mess. We like ta take care uh our own, but we just-"

"It's ok Meeka. We want the shatterheads. You don't need to pay us," assures Alice, getting a look from Danahlia.

Meeka brightens considerably at this, "Oh, that is just wonderful to hear, and there's plenty of 'em. You will not go wantin' for those critters, that's a promise. Why I heard they could gather in the hundreds if the mood strikes 'em. I am so glad I found y'all. It was fate, I know it, led me right to ya. Moment I saw you three with 'em-"

Danahlia cuts her off this time, "Hey Twi- uh Amber, what's that book o' yours say about the shatterheads?"

The girls had come up with aliases for themselves so their true names wouldn't leave a trail. Twinkaleni was now Amber Grayfur.

Claiming to have committed her entire bestiary/herbiary to memory, Twinkaleni doesn't need to pull out the large tome from her pack, "There was an extensive entry on them, rather interesting. As you mentioned before, the shatterheads have a particularly rigid snout, thick with bone. They use this in combination with a charge in order to build momentum that allows them to head-butt their enemies with devastating force. Capable of weighing several hundred pounds, they are well known for shattering the shin bones and knees of those unlucky enough to be on the receiving end of such an attack, hence their name. Their diet consists of anything they can find, primarily plants, roots, and berries, but they have also been seen eating eggs, small animals, and even reptiles when they can catch them."

Twinkaleni, never one to shy away from explanations, goes on in length about the creatures. Hearing about them makes Alice feel more prepared but also a little more anxious. From what Twinkaleni says, shatterheads are normally solitary creatures, their aggressive tendencies making them think of anything, even their own kind, as enemies, though when food is abundant they can gather in large roving hoards. Meeka chimes in frequently, confirming Twikaleni's data with her own experience with the beasts.

Together, the girls come up with various strategies and tactics they believe will work against the shatterheads, ones that combine their new spears, Twinkaleni's magic, and a few arrows. They walk beside the slow moving wagon to practice some, Alice and Danahlia thrusting and moving about with their new weapons to get a feel for them. A problem Meeka presents is that when provoked in groups, the shatterheads have been known to band together temporarily to defend themselves, causing dangerous collective charges. From her own experiences with the boars, Twinkaleni feels confident that her fire magic will prevent this but is sure to develop strategies that ward against it.

Lost in concocting various plans for a time, the girls don't realize they've arrived in the farmlands until Meeka looks around and announces, "We're… here."

Chapter 4

Pig Hunt

Surrounded by fence, some parts of it knocked over or broken, are the remains of once tilled fields, stamped flat and eaten lifeless by the shatterheads. A handful of the ferals still nuzzle the dirt in the distance, perhaps seeking a few leftover tubers. A lone farm house sits in the center of the barren plot of land, dark and silent in defeat.

"Oh no, this is terrible. This used to be a potatah field, all of it. The shatterheads hadn't touched it when I left," says Meeka.

"When was that?" asks Twinkaleni.

Meeka, clearly distressed, replies, "I headed on into Barley just three days ago."

"They cleared this whole place in three days?" asks Alice, astonished.

Meeka nods, "Looks like. We gotta get to mah farm quick," then to Lulu she asks, "Can't this thing go any faster?"

The donkey is uninterested in increasing its pace and Lulu suggests, "You can probably walk faster, I'll catch up."

The girls gather their things and quickly outpace the wagon. Meeka calls back to Lulu, "Mine's the second field up on this road and to the left, yella' house." Then she begins to jog.

The girls keep with her until they start to see more shatterheads. They're mostly concentrated in a field to the right side of the road, devouring what look like pumpkins or some other large gourdes. A small group of people are out waving hoes and various farm tools at them to little effect, getting only a few to run off only to have them quickly rejoin the feeding frenzy.

"Let's get 'em!" shouts Danahlia, dropping her backpack against a low fence and then leaping over it, both her spears in hand. Alice does the same, taking her bow, arrows, spear, and sword.

Twinkaleni can't get over or through the fence and has to run around to a break in it as she calls, "Tanya! Master! Wait!" Alice was Tanya Softpaw and Danahlia was Master Denelia Thrashtail when anyone besides the trio was present.

Alice turns, and sees Meeka running off along the road calling back, "I gotta check on my momma!"

Danahlia charges toward a lone shatterhead, spears raised, as Alice and Twinkaleni move to get in range of the larger gatherings. Alice kneels, placing her melee weapons on the ground and knocks an arrow. She aims at the center mass of the ravenous hogs and lets loose. A high squeal tells her she made a hit, setting those around it into a confused panic, scattering the beasts. Alice continues firing at the fleeing individuals as Twinakleni begins casting beams of fire in an effort to force them away from the still uneaten crop fields and back into the barren ones.

Seeing this, the farmers rally to join in the attack, finishing shatterheads that were knocked down by their panicked kin, while shouting and chasing after the rest. Alice sees Danahlia throw her crab leg spear into one of the beasts as it runs by and it falls, tumbling into the dirt. The Liguna then thrusts her boar spear into the downed pig about where Artyom said its heart would be. She retrieves the thrown spear and quickly moves on to another. Alice takes down a shatterhead with arrows, wounding and slowing a handful more. Once she's out, Alice drops her bow, takes up her spear, and begins to follow Danahlia's example.

She's lining up a thrust with one of the beasts fleeing in her general direction, when she hears a farmer call, "Look out!"

Alice misses her chance, the boar running past her, but she turns to find another particularly large one charging for Twinkaleni. Alice tries to turn around, but the loose dirt causes her to slip and slide to one knee. She cries warning to the Murin who only now notices the large shatterhead barreling toward her, an arrow sticking out of its side.

Twinkaleni ceases the beam of fire she was throwing at some others to turn to the charging beast. Then, with one hand rising before her, she calls out, "Asendiote!" The large shatterhead begins to float as it runs for her, its momentum causing it to sail well over her head. When it gets a few yards past her, Twinkaleni shouts, "Gravitus!" and flings her tiny upraised hand to the ground.

The boar crashes to the earth with a magnificent thud and doesn't rise from its plume of dust. After using so much magic, Alice expects the diminutive girl to collapse in exhaustion but instead she simply turns to find more targets. Impressed by the mage's ever growing power, Alice moves on to finish some of the wounded beasts, the rest having run too far off to be of concern.

She confronts one, still standing with an arrow in its hind leg and another in its ribs. It turns to her, too wounded to run and to stubborn to die. The shatterhead threatens with angry grunts as it scrapes the earth with a forehoof keeping Alice before it even as she tries to get an angle on its weak spot. Seeing the creature limping as she tries to finish it starts to bring on guilt and for a bizarre moment she considers trying to tell it to just let her end it's suffering. She's about to strike it in the face, when a pitch fork is driven into its side, followed by a little Leeseran. The beast topples over but the young squirrel boy doesn't release the pitch fork and ends up falling over it. Worried the boy might get hurt, Alice swiftly steps up to the shatterhead and drives her spear into its heart, or where she is fairly sure it's supposed to be. Leaving the spear there, she grabs the back of the boy's shirt and pulls him away from the still kicking hog. They both fall to their butts in the dirt.

"Are you ok?" Alice asks the boy, looking him over while ignoring the throb of her squished tail. Alice guesses he is perhaps eight or nine years of age as he gives her a shaky nod and watches the shatterhead slow until it ceases it's kicks.

"That was pretty brave," says Danahlia, coming over to pull Alice to her feet. The boy smiles but then looks frightened when Danahlia offers him a clawed hand.

He pulls away, "What are you?"

Danahlia frowns, "I'm one of the ones who just saved your farm."

"Hey! You get away from 'im!" shouts a thin Leeseran man, hobbling toward them on crutches, a hoe in one hand.

A rather robust Leeseran woman follows him, catching the man when he nearly tumbles and scolds, "Marmin, now you stop it."

"I don't want no egger anywhere near mah boy!" the man, Marmin, shouts, regaining his balance. Alice notices the man doesn't have a tail, Leeserans typically having particularly long, poofy ones.

"Marmin!" the woman shouts.

"Egger?" Alice asks, getting the boy to his feet.

"A derogatory term for the cold blooded," Twinkaleni supplies, joining them, "Pay it no mind, Master Thrashtail. The man clearly does not recognize who you are."

Danahlia wears the red cloak of the Order but much of it, including the hood, has fallen behind her. She adjusts it, letting the long fabric flow over her shoulders and puts up the hood, grumbling, "If this is how you treat the ones who risked themselves to save your crops, we'll be sure to let the shatterheads have 'em next time."

Marmin snarls, "Ah don't need no help from no filthy, egg layin', puddle hopper!"

"THAT IS ENOUGH!" the woman bellows, "Cordi, take you father inside this instant, he's clearly too tired to be civil."

"Don't tell me what's what woman, hey, get off me boy!" the man argues, squirming weakly as Cordi gently guides his father back around to a small house.

"I am *so* sorry dear," the woman apologizes, trying to reach for Danahlia, but the Liguna pulls

away, turning and stomping off in the opposite direction. "Oh, never you mind what that old fool says, oh," the Leeseran calls, raising a hand regretfully after her.
Surprised by the reaction, Alice watches her friend storm off only to suddenly hurl her boar spear far into the field. She and Twinkaleni follow her as the woman calls to them, "I'm so sorry, please don't judge him too harshly. It's what the war done to 'im."

Alice glances back, seeing the woman looking after them, and then turns to her friend, "What's wrong?"

Danahlia paces, her tail held high and stiff with agitation, but says, "Nothin'," with a sniff.

Alice maneuvers in front of her, putting a hand on the taller girl's shoulder. Danahlia looks sharply away but Alice catches a glimpse of a tear in her eye.

Danahlia turns from her, shaking her head, "It's people," another sniff, "It's people like *him*," she takes a few rapid breathes, "that ruined EVERYTHING!" She screams the last into the open field, startling Alice.

The few other farmers that were approaching, stop. After a silent moment, Danahlia starts toward where she hurled her boar spear, shaking her head some more with a deep frown. Alice and Twinkaleni follow her. Unsure of what else to say, Alice tries to apologize for the squirrel man's behavior though Twinkaleni stays silent.

Danahlia sniffs again, "Naw, let's just get our kills and go." She rips the spear from the earth and walks toward one of the dead shatterheads, the farmers looking on.

Alice and Twinkaleni take a side each and try to comfort their companion. As they're dragging the shatterheads to the road, Twinkaleni explains that many cold blooded people lay eggs to reproduce. This is unlike mammals, such as Alice and herself, but similar to the Avian peoples who have, and generally do, ally with the other Warm Bloods in times of conflict. She says this to emphasize the foolishness of using egg laying as an insult to Cold Bloods when it also insults Warm Blood allies.

Twinkaleni then attacks the notion of Danahlia being a "puddle hopper," saying while it is true that many Cold Bloods like the water, this is a reference that should only apply to Amphibious peoples, not Reptilians like Danahlia, who prefer the land. She goes on to say that the man is clearly lacking in education for having made such poorly considered accusations.

The other farmers keep a generous distance, perhaps made wary by Danahlia's outburst or Twinkaleni's magic, but call their thanks. They also tell them that the shatterheads routed here were only a fraction of the horde that still ravages the farmlands.

Lulu catches up to them and they determine the wagon can only hold five shatterheads while still being able to move. The girls defeated nine and tell the farmers they can have the rest, for which they are grateful, knowing they can either sell or eat the beasts themselves. Alice recovers what arrows she can, though several have broken on impact or when a struck shatterhead fell on them. Danahlia's crab leg spear was also crushed under a fallen boar.

Even so, they consider this a victory, and when Meeka returns the girls follow her to her family's cabbage patch. They arrive far too late, nearly all the crop already devoured, but bring down two of the few remaining shatterheads with arrows and a well-placed thrust from Danahlia's boar spear. The others flee from the Lotarin's land and the raccoon girl and her mother thank the trio. By then, it's well into the afternoon and after a short break, they and Lulu begin the trip back to Barley, assuring the farmers that they will return tomorrow. The walk to town is slow and exhausting but the time passes faster as the girls regale Lulu with their stories of the day's battles. Lulu tells them that Barley is likely to have a smith that may be able to replace Danahlia's spear, but says they should ask Artyom to be sure.

The small party is glad, and a bit surprised, when they finally arrive back at the Bear's Den near dusk. As they enter, they find the inn packed with customers, sitting and standing, all enjoying bowls of stew.

Artyom, Misha, and even little Lolo are busy serving but that doesn't stop the massive Urock man from calling cheerfully, "Hehey girls! What I tell you?! Artyom's stew is famous!"

The bear man waves for them to follow him into the kitchen where they find Levi atop a barrel of ale, turning the spigot to fill mugs whenever Misha or Lolo place one under it. Artyom gives them all a generous helping of stew and they start to eat gluttonously while they tell him how the day's hunt went. He's overjoyed to hear they brought five pigs back and as he hauls them through the main hall from the wagon, he announces there will be plenty more shatterhead stew, getting an enthusiastic cheer from his patrons.

He offers the girls the same room from the night before and another fat purse filled with coins. He also buys all of Lulu's carrots for a nice sum. As he hands her the coins, Alice offers her seven shils, the price for one of the hogs, as payment for driving the wagon for them. Lulu gratefully accepts and moves on to see to her two children.

The girls ask Artyom about finding a smith to replace Danahlia's broken spear. He informs them that there is only one left in town, many of the rest having been conscripted by the military to make arms and armor for the war. He says the smith is an old Echanian who, despite his age, is skilled and should be able to provide what the girls are after, for a price. They make plans to visit him in the morning and take their stew upstairs to their room, leaving the crowded hall below.

Dumping the purse on the floor to count out their new finances, Danahlia exclaims, "Wags! We're rich!"

"Shhh!" Twinkaleni squeaks, "Have you learned nothing? Who knows who could be listening in on us even here, even now."

Danahlia largely ignores her, picking up handfuls of coins to shower them onto the others with satisfying little clinks. These added to what the girls already had makes them feel rather proud of themselves.

"How much do you think a spear costs?" wonders Alice.

Danahlia grins at all their silver, "I don't know, but with all this, I don't think we have to worry about price."

"Tweny-five shils?! You gotta be freakin' kiddin'!" shouts Danahlia, the next morning at Mr. Gifer's forge.

The old, gray coated, white maned Echanian crosses his arms over his chest, both still thick with muscle despite his advanced years, "You wanna decent boar spear, that's what it'll cost ya."

"Come on guys, this old hoofers tryin' to rip us off," Danahlia grumbles, turning back to the street.

"Heh, and go where? Mine's the only hammer left in town," Mr. Gifer tosses back, his voice still deep and strong.

Twinkaleni tries to reason, "Your price seems a bit disproportionate to our order, sir. Surely you would do more business if you balance your labor costs more evenly with your fee."

"Boar spears tweny-five shils. Ya aint got it, then move along, I got work to do," the Echanian stubbornly replies.

"Please sir, we need it to hunt the shatterheads that are ravagin' the farmland around Barley," pleads Alice, "Without the farms' harvests, no one's gonna have anythin' to eat, includin' you."

"Hmm, so you're the ones been supplyin' the hogs over at Artyom's, eh? Why didn't ya say so? Thirty shils," the man replies.

"WHAT?!" Danahlia shouts, turning sharply.

"I reckon huntin' shatterheads can be a *mighty* profitable endeavor with all the folk lookin' to buy meat. I'm sure you girls are gettin' your fair share o' coin. You should consider it an investment in your huntin' business. Plus, I don't need nobody thinkin' I'm given a smoothie any kinda special treatment, even if ye' are from that order."

This tips Danahlia over and she begins stomping over to the man, Artyom's boar spear held high, "Why you, *greedy* ol-!"

"Ngh, Danny stop! Let's just pay him," says Alice, pushing against the enraged Liguna's chest while Twinkaleni grabs a leg, trying to keep her from getting to the smirking horse man.

"What?! He's totally rippin' us off!" Danahlia exclaims.

"I know, he *is*," agrees Alice with a pointed glance at the man, "But you need a new spear, we have the money, let's just get one and go."

Danahlia clenches her jaw and looks like she wants to spit in the man's smirking face, but eventually lets Twinkaleni take her outside. As Alice is handing the man his money he tells her to come back tomorrow for it, but before she can leave, Danahlia shouts back in, "This better be the best spear ever made!"

Mr. Gifer just grins at all the silver in his hands.

That day, the girls go back out into the farmlands to hunt shatterheads with Lulu and her wagon. They find a group of farmers out trying to fend off the beasts from another plot. There are even more wild hogs and a few more farmers this time. Some are ones the trio helped yesterday and these wave them over. It seems the farmers from other properties are banding together to try to drive off the hungry ferals from a large patch of something green and leafy. From the bare patches behind the ravenous creatures, it's plain to see the farmers are steadily being pushed back. Joining their strife, the girls watch as pitchforks, scythes, and hoes scare a few of the closest but even so, the sheer number of oncoming shatterheads keeps their lines pushing forward despite wounds and casualties.

The trio takes position on a small hill and begin their attack, Danahlia launching a few fireballs from her ring while Alice looses arrows and Twinkaleni unleashes her magic upon them. It has the desired effect, causing the animals to squeal and scatter in all directions, letting the farmers and the girls pick off a few of the panicked beasts while frightening away the majority. After her previous success, Twinkaleni begins lifting boars with her earth magic to hurl them at others with stunning force, leaving them vulnerable to Danahlia and

Alice's spears. Lifting such heavy beasts repeatedly exhausts the small mage but many shatterheads are defeated for her efforts, much to the appreciation of the defending farmers.

After the battle, a few even help load up Lulu's wagon with the girl's due five, asking that they come back to liberate their own lands from the hog menace. The girls agree to this and taking a break, watch as another larger wagon, this one pulled by two horses, is loaded with many of the remaining downed shatterheads. The driver says he's planning to sell them in town as the girls are. With the money, the farmers hope to be able to better prepare for the coming winter season.

That night at the Bear's Den, as the trio is settling into their beds, Alice once more lying with Danahlia, the lizard girl says, "This is kinda nice. We go out, we take down a few pigs, save a few farms, and then we come back here and get paid."

"Yeah," nods Alice, shimming under the sheets.

"I agree. We're getting a great deal of training in. Your archery skills have improved significantly, Alice," says Twinkaleni.

Alice turns to smile at the little mouse in the opposite bed, "Thanks. And your magic is getting really powerful."

The Murin mage grins, "Mmm, perhaps."

Danahlia looks over Alice's head at the small girl, the breath from her words making the Tokala's ears twitch, "It's true, you were tossin' pigs all over today and didn't even pass out."

Twinkaleni's grin widens, "I do admit, I have been feeling a bit more capable. Though I would like us to practice our close quarters combat techniques more often."

"Why? Your magic seems like it suits you better," says Alice.

"I've told you before, the Order of Thermathrogi is well versed in dealing with magical threats. Therefore, I must learn alternative fighting methods if I am to be of any use in an attack," explains Twinkaleni.

Danahlia snorts, making Alice's ears twitch again, "You're still goin' on about that? Besides, don't you think you're a little short to be fightin' up close?"

The little mouse huffs, rolling away from them and then over her shoulder says, "On the contrary, I believe my size could be an asset if used properly. I may not know much about facing an enemy directly, but I do know that smaller targets are harder to hit."

Alice jabs Danahlia in the stomach with an elbow. Ignoring the Liguna's sound of protest, the fox girl whispers, "You know this means a lot to her, we should be supportive," then to Twinkaleni she says, "Yeah, we can do some more sparring, right Danny?"

Danahlia, rubbing her tummy, grumbles, "Yeah, fine. We'll get some in soon, maybe tomorrow."

With that, the girls snuggle up, say their good nights, and drift off.

Sometime after, Alice is awoken by Twinkaleni mumbling in her sleep. After a few moments, Alice realizes the little mage is muttering, "It's my fault, all my fault," over and over. Danahlia hears it too and as they make their way to Twinkaleni's bed, the tiny girl wakes with a sharp inhale, eyes wide, a subtle golden glow fading in them as she shivers.

Alice and Danahlia lie down on either side of her, holding and stroking her soft fur. She doesn't protest and together they fall back to sleep.

The next day, the trio heads back to Mr. Gifer's forge for their spear. They're somewhat surprised to find it's exactly what Danahlia had wanted. The haft is thinner and lighter than that of Artyom's while still being sturdy. The blade and wings are similarly thinner, with the blade sharpened to a razor edge.

Danahlia twirls the blade before her eyes, pursing her lips, "Not bad."

"Not bad?" the smith rumbles, arms crossing over his large chest, though he can't suppress a prideful smirk, "That's a two inch center cut Alcina haft and a Chilalan steel head, you're lucky I had one in stock."

The words mean little to Alice but Twinkaleni nods, "Impressive. Hypothetically, were I in need of arms, what would you recommend?"

Mr. Gifer grins down at the tiny Murin, "I recommend you grow about five feet." Twinkaleni narrows her eyes at him and his grin subsides, "I've made Murin weapons before. Folk from all over, even nobles, used to come to me to forge 'em anything you can think of for figthin' this or huntin' that. You girls need to count yourselves lucky twice for havin' access to such a talented man."

"If you're so talented, why'd the army take all the smiths but you?" asks Alice.

The Echanian snorts, "Said I was too old. Can you believe that? I can forge a sword o' better quality in half the time it'd take anyone half my age. Too old. Said the town needed at least one smith, might as well be me. Idiots."

"Indeed, now about my request," says Twinkaleni.

The Echanian looks over to her from where he turned to a hoe he seemed to be mending, "Right, what you need it for?"

"General protection I suppose," replies the Murin.

"I got somethin' in mind. Come back in about a week, might have somethin' for ya then."

Chapter 5

Fame and Infamy

Nearly a month is spent in Barley, the girls chasing off shatterheads during the day and staying at the Bear's Den at night, training when they can. True to his word, on their next visit, Mr. Gifer had prepared a set of small blades for Twinkaleni. One he calls a rapier, a slender needle like sword fitting to the Murin's diminutive size, and the other he says is a main gauche, a dagger with a slightly wider, if significantly shorter, blade. Both have wide curved guards he claims will aid in catching an enemies' blade as well as protect her delicate little fingers. He charges a great deal for these, but with their funds from selling shatterheads, the girls can more than cover it.

Unexpectedly, the trio's almost daily arrival in the besieged countryside is soon greeted with growing cheers from the embattled farmers. After aiding so many by routing the menacing boars and leaving many of those they defeat to the farmers for their own sustenance and profit, the girls have developed a bit of a reputation as local heroes. Praises are also commonly given in the Order of Thermathrogi's name for having sent them, a falsehood true, but one the trio had no intention of correcting.

The girls are heading out again with Lulu. Passing by previously cleared fields, they're waved at and called to by grateful farmers busily trying to get things back in order. With each victory, the shatterheads are pushed further back out into open country and the donkey pulled wagon must travel a little farther. This means the trip back to Barley is that much longer as well, and because of this, Lulu often takes the girl's share of the defeated wild boars back without them. The farmers are generally more than happy to put them up, hoping they'll be around to ward off more attacks by the ever ravenous ferals. After a particularly well earned victory, a feast of barbecued shatterhead is held to celebrate. While Artyom's stew is excellent, something about flame roasted shatterhead ribs make these feasts something to look forward to.

Approaching a crossroads, Lulu says she sees something ahead. The girls peek over to find a heap of clothes along the side of the road that turns out to be a person, a person with a long, furless, green tail.

Danahlia leaps to the ground and runs to them calling, "Sister!" Confused, Alice and Twinkaleni look on from the still moving wagon. As Danahlia reaches the prone figure, she kneels, "Hey, are you ok?"

A throaty feminine voice emerges from the figure as it turns to Danahlia, a few bits of her loose clothes falling away to reveal another female Liguna, "Oh, hello little lashtail."

Physically, she looks very similar to Danahlia though with more matured features and lime green skin. As Lulu brings the wagon to a halt, Alice leaps off to get a closer look, this only being the second Cold Blood she had ever seen. Twinkaleni remains in the wagon, large ears perked in interest. The woman props herself on her elbows while Danahlia gives her a strong hug. The woman seems surprised by this but then puts an arm over her younger kin. Over Danahlia's shoulder, the woman watches Alice approach.

She doesn't look hurt and something in the woman's eyes makes the young Tokala pause before asking, "Are you ok? What're you doin' out here in the open?"

"Why, we're here to collect a toll," she says, a devious grin spreading across her face.

"What?" Danahlia asks, pulling away from her.

Alice looks around and then back at the woman, her head cocking to one side. The Liguna woman looks around too and then calls much louder, "I said, we're here to collect a *toll*!"

Only then do several more figures emerge from the tall grass a little ways off, though one has managed to creep up behind the wagon. They all wear grasses over their skin, but Alice can clearly see that all three are Cold Bloods. The one that emerged from behind them is large with thick muscles and looks rather different from a Liguna. His sand tan skin appears much rougher and he has small horns protruding from his neck up to his crown. Worse, he's armed with a club. Twinkaleni faces him from atop the wagon pulling free her tiny rapier and main gauche.

Lulu nervously takes up Danahlia's boar spear from where it was left in the bed of her wagon muttering, "Bandits."

Hearing this, Alice is about to draw her sword when a warning of, "I wouldn't do that if I were you," comes to her from another male Cold Blood, this one aiming an arrow at her from behind a drawn bow. As he makes his way toward her, careful to keep her in his sights, Alice can see this one has a swampy green coloring with dark stripes and looks similar but clearly isn't a Liguna. He has a slender muzzle but a wide jaw, and when he grins she can see it's filled with jagged, short teeth. Atop his head and along his throat are a single row of backward facing spikes that look more fleshy than rigid. Alice doesn't move but can see the fourth maneuvering to her left around the wagon, this one, a male Liguna of brown and yellow wielding a knife.

The woman pushes Danahlia behind her as she rises, revealing her own dagger, "Just stay behind me and you'll be safe."

"What? But these are my friends," Danahlia protests, getting a look from the others.

Not eager to know what an arrow to the chest feels like, Alice calls, still looking at the archer with one hand on Jellybane's handle, "You said you wanted a toll?"

"That's right, Furface," sneers the archer, "We'll be takin' those weapons off your hands and anything else you got in the wagon. Scratch that, just leave everything in the wagon, we'll be havin' that too."

"By what right do you charge a toll here?" inquires Twinkleni, her rapier pointed at the largest Cold Blood, who just smiles at the tiny Murin.

"Ears that big and you haven't 'eard? I and my merry band have taken this crossroad in the name of glorious Feoria," the archer claims in a proud tone, "It is ours by right of conquest, and passage through carries the toll of coin or blood. Which is it gonna be?"

"Stop this! These are good people," says Danahlia from behind the woman.

The male Liguna carrying the knife and watching Lulu calls to the lizard woman, "Careful, Beryl. Think this one's gone furry, might even have some hairs growin' under that cloak o' hers."

"Nah, she's alright. Just been around these furbacks so long she forgot who her real friends were," the woman replies, "Isn't that right, little lashtail?"

Unarmed, Danahlia says nothing but looks to Alice and then significantly at the archer. As he orders them to surrender their weapons again, Alice gives a slight nod. Understanding that Danahlia is about to make a move, Alice tightens her grip on her sword.

"I mean *now,* girl!" the archer says, pulling his bow to a full draw.

The archer takes a step forward, drawing the woman's gaze to Alice. Danahlia uses this to shove the Liguna woman as hard as she can into the archer. The woman falls over the man with a surprised cry and the arrow flies free. It zips past Alice close enough that she can feel the fur part beside her cheek. Before the man can react, Alice has her sword at his throat as Danahlia lands on the woman's back, pinning her to the ground and over the archer's legs.

Lulu keeps the knife wielding Liguna at bay with waves of Danahlia's boar spear and they all hear Twinkaleni call, "Asendiote!"

Alice doesn't turn away from the archer, trusting in her friends. But then a wildly moving shadow falls over her and the archer looks wide-eyed past her. Alice can't help glancing over her shoulder then, to see the largest Cold Blood flailing in the air and crying for help just before Twinkaleni shouts, "Telefuss!"

The command sends the large man screaming into the knife wielding Liguna, taking them both hard to the ground. Alice grins back at the archer, his mouth open in shock.

Then, with a call of, "Feasta!" the Murin rakes a beam of fire over everyone's heads before ordering, "Disarm and desist or perish."

"A witch," the archer snarls but drops his bow, arrows, and a small dagger. The other bandits let go of their weapons as well and the girls have them gather together in the middle of the road.

Collecting their arms, Danahlia asks, "Why are you robbin' people out here?"

"We don't answer to traitors," spits the male Liguna.

"I'm not a traitor!" growls Danahlia.

"You attack your own people and turn them in to these mangy hair-hides? Sounds like a traitor to me," the same one grumbles.

"*You* attacked *us*!" shouts Alice, sword drawn and aimed at the bunch.

"You're the bandits that have been causing so much trouble around Barley," claims Lulu, still wielding Danahlia's boar spear.

"Maybe. What's it to you, long ear?" grumbles the former archer.

"Do you have any idea of how bad you're makin' things for the rest of us?! As If our people didn't have enough to worry about, you're just makin' it worse!" Danahlia shouts angrily.

After a moment's silence the large one that Twinkaleni threw mumbles, "Didn't want to be bandits. Just got tired o' hidin', o' beggin', o' livin' every day in fear." His eyes stare intently on the ground before him in shame.

"We're not bandits!" the woman snarls at the large man, "We're freedom fighters."

"You're nothing but common rouges, taking advantage of desperate people during a desperate time. Your actions not only condemn you but others of your kind," says Twinkaleni.

"We're NOT-" the woman says again rising, but stops when Alice's sword tip pans to her face.

Another silence and the archer asks Danahlia, "What do you plan to do with us?"

The girls look to each other. They have no rope to tie them up with and turning them in to the locals would surely mean death for them all. As they consider silently, they hear a rumbling from a ways off and look down one of the other roads to a wagon with a handful of farmers heading right for them. The Cold Bloods see this and tense.

Danahlia tosses a bow and one of the smaller knives to them, "There's a large forest to the south. We know there's food and water, you can make a go of it there." They look up to her in confusion and she shouts, "Go! And if I hear you've been robbin' people again, we'll hunt you down and let the Warm Bloods have you!"

"You're letting them go?" asks Lulu, keeping the boar spear raised defensively.

"Do you really want their blood on your hands?" replies Danahlia, while the four snatch up the weapons and begin running in the opposite direction of the oncoming wagon.

The woman, Beryl, turns back, extending a hand to Danahlia, "Come with us. You belong with your own people."

To Alice's surprise, Danahlia actually seems to consider this and when she looks back to her, Alice gives her friend a pleading shake of her head.

Danahlia turns to the woman, waving her off, "I'm stayin' here, go!"

The woman appears to want to press the issue but sees the wagon is closing fast and turns to race after her companions.

Danahlia sighs heavily, looking after them until the large wagon, pulled by a team of horses, stops before them. Some of the farmers recognize the girls and ask what had happened. They tell them that the bandits troubling the area won't be anymore, showing them the small cache of weapons they had collected. Pleased with the news, the driver tells them that she's heading for a pasture that's been overrun with shatterheads and asks the girls to join them. They decide to follow the farmers on Lulu's wagon.

The trio sits in silence until Alice can hold back no longer and asks, "Were you really thinkin' about goin' with 'em?"

Danahlia, sitting beside her, looks to the fox girl, "What? No, no, come on, what would you guys do without me?" She then looks at some middle distance, "It's just, been a while, you know?" after a few seconds she adds, "It was kinda nice to see that there're still some of us out here. Maybe we'll find some who aren't thieves and you can see what good, honest Cold Bloods are really like."

Alice places her head on the lizard girl's shoulder, "I'm glad you didn't go."

"As am I," assures Twinkaleni, looking out over the side of the wagon.

"Yeah," Danahlia returns, resting her head over Alice's and rubbing a cheek over one of her ears.

The pasture is on the outer rim of the farmlands and as they travel, the larger wagon stops to pick up other people heading that way. Everyone who joins is armed with everything from various farming tools to sharpened sticks and knives. Meeka and her mother are among them, and the raccoon girl joins the trio in Lulu's wagon. She tells them that they sold the shatterheads the trio left after liberating her small cabbage patch and got a decent some in Barley. Since then, she and her mother have been heading out to aid other farms, hoping to collect more valuable meat. She has only a long sharpened stick and a knife with her, so the girls give her two of the heftier weapons seized from the bandits.

Approaching the pasture, the girls can see people on foot heading in the same direction. Eventually they come to a stop among a few other wagons. Farmers and townsfolk have gathered into a large crowd, eager for a chance to bring down shatterheads of their own. Standing atop Lulu's wagon, the four girls look far into the rolling hills and flat meadows to a veritable sea of wild hogs. Their coarse brown coats let the ferals blend into one another, making them look like one massive entity. Further out from the main mass are smaller patches of brown, and further still are a few individuals some people have already taken to hunting. Most of the people gathered though, seem to be waiting for something.

"I can't see, what's happening?" says Twinkaleni, standing on her toes.

Danahlia picks the tiny Murin up and places her on her shoulders as Alice points to the hog covered hills, "Look at 'em all."

The girls had thought they had been routing the shatterheads and pushing them back, but seeing their true numbers makes it abundantly clear that their previous battles with the beasts had all been minor skirmishes at best.

"How can there still be so many?" wonders Meeka.

Twinkaleni, holding onto Danahlia's neck with one hand and shielding her eyes from the sun with the other, replies, "Perhaps all of the fleeing shatterheads have congregated here, feeling more secure in their numbers. If this is so, a victory in these pastures may finally end the threat."

"Got anythin' for handlin' this many?" Danahlia asks up to her.

"If you are referring to magic, then no, but-"

Before the small girl can go on, people around the wagon begin to call, "It's them!"

Alice looks around the seventy or so people who have gathered and sees they're looking up at her and her friends.

Voices ring out over the crowd, "It's them! The ones sent by the Order!"

Others claim, "They've come to lead us!"

And someone calls, "Finally, let's get these pigs off our land!"

The crowd bursts into excitement, weapons rising as bodies begin to press up against the wagon.

Alice steps back from the edge, "Oh, ticks, I think they're talkin' about us."

The wagon begins to shift under the pressure of so many people and Danahlia starts to wobble. Twinkaleni, atop her, holds on tightly to her neck so she doesn't fall.

"Ugh, loosen... Twin-guh, you're choking meh..." Danahlia croaks as Alice raises her arms in the air as she had seen some do when addressing a gathering. Slowly the wagon stills and the crowd goes silent.

Not really sure what to do next, Alice just stands there, her arms still help high, looking at all the faces peering up at her.

"Say somethin'," Meeka presses but under all those demanding gazes, Alice's tail tucks and she can't think of a single word.

"How do we beat the shatterheads?!" a woman cries.

"Can we beat 'em? There're so many!" another shouts.

"They're just ferals!" is countered by, "Have you seen what they can do to you!?"

Arguments begin to break out as Danahlia lifts the Murin mage off of her shoulders. "Uh-oh, we're losin' 'em. Quick do some fire," suggests Danahlia, giving the Murin a shake.

Still in the Liguna's arms, Twinkaleni extends a finger and shouts "Feasta!" She pans a beam of orange flame over the crowd, bringing a few startled cries but then silence.

"Ok, all yours, Alice," says Danahlia stepping back with Twinkaleni.

"What? Why me?" Alice protests, trying to step back too, but Meeka holds her steady.

"You can do it. Just tell 'em how we're gonna kick those pigs off our land and make lots o' money doin' it!" the Lotarin girl encourages.

"Uh," is all Alice can manage and the crowd begins to murmur.

Trying again, Alice says, "So, we're all here to fight the shatterheads, right?"

A few people respond in agreement while a man grumbles, "Well, we ain't here tah throw 'em a party."

He gets a laugh or two and Alice nods, "Right! We're here to beat those pigs back!"

More people shout their approval.

"We're here to take back our land!" shouts Alice.

She gets a cheer of, "Yeah!"

"We're here to stick those pigs and eat 'em!" adds Danahlia to another cheer.

"And sell'em!" shouts Meeka, getting another.

After a short silence a Leeseran woman asks, "So, how do we?"

"Uh, well-," Alice starts only to be cut off by Twinkaleni.

"I believe I have a strategy that will allow us..." Danahlia places the small girl atop her shoulders once again, "...us to eradicate the shatterhead threat as safely and efficiently as possible." The Murin pauses for a moment to be sure she has everyone's attention, "We have seen to great effect the efficiency of fire as a charge deterrent and scattering mechanism. I propose we use the beasts' inherent aversion to flame to segregate more feasible groups from the primary conglomeration. Repeated destruction of these isolated cells will slowly diminish their numbers until the shatterheads are defeated!" shouts Twinkaleni, raising a tiny fist.

The crowd stares blankly and someone calls, "Whut?!"

"We'll use fire to separate 'em into smaller groups and beat 'em one group at a time," clarifies Danahlia, and the people cheer once more.

Having seen the effectiveness of fire, many farmers had brought torches but Twinkaleni feels it is nowhere near enough and asks that dried hay, straw, and other flammable materials be brought. She also advises wood be cut and shaped into spears to help supply the poorly equipped militia. Many of the gathered people are too impatient for this and form smaller parties to join others already in the field engaging the shatterheads furthest from the main mass. Seeing their early success, those not occupied with a task become restless and the girls lead them to begin preliminary attacks.

The shatterheads are spread over an expansive area and Twinkaleni uses her fire magic to force a few away from the larger groupings. The mob of peasants quickly descends upon these, dispatching them with zeal, if little tact. Those slain are immediately set upon as claims over the kills and meat are made. Some pigs are haphazardly butchered right there in the grass under arguing throngs who practically tear the creatures apart. The girls try to stop these with promises of great quantities of meat for everyone, pointing out that there are still hundreds of shatterheads to fell. Still, a couple of those who have claimed generous portions of meat already begin the long trip back to Barley, eager to sell.

They do this several times, taking dozens of boars, but running into the same problem. Twinkaleni suggests they wait until after the battle is over to divide the spoils evenly, but the idea gets little support. It seems the townsfolk are far more interested in claiming meat than clearing land and it's mostly they who argue, take, and leave. Fortunately, most that have congregated are farmers and their louder voice helps keep the people together. Even so, after mounting jealousy over the townspeople taking all the meat, some farmers begin taking the pigs from the field and piling them with those sharpening more spears to guard for later dispersal. All these acts whittle away at the attacking force and continue to lower the odds of success. Meanwhile, the shatterheads gorge themselves, paying little interest unless directly provoked.

As the day wains and bodies sag with exhaustion, large pyres are built and tended to over the newly taken pasture lands to keep the shatterheads from reclaiming them in the night. This doesn't seem entirely necessary, however, as many of the wild ferals move off to wherever they keep coming from to rest.

Tensions ebb when part of the day's take is butchered and placed over the fire for all to enjoy. Many more leave then, taking their shares, but plenty stay and the day's success is celebrated with music, dancing, singing, and great boasting of individual hunting prowess. Many thanks are given to the trio, especially Twinkaleni, whose use of fire magic is praised frequently. Lulu has left with a few shatterheads, not wanting to spend the night without her children. Tired, the girls eat their fill of pork and quickly go to sleep beside one of the pyres.

The next day, the shatterheads have returned and so have many of the townsfolk. Word spreads that the price for shatterhead meat is diminishing with the influx in Barley's market and people are more eager than ever to get larger sums. This leads to more aggressive hunting. And now that the people are better equipped with spears and flammable bundles of dry grasses, hay, and straw, Twinkaleni proposes a bold new strategy.

Those with pitchforks, and other tools capable of the task, are assigned into teams to carry burning bundles forward to scare the shatterheads. When a sizable group has broken off from the main horde, Twinkaleni lays down literal cover fire while the fire carriers set down their bundles to form flaming barriers that keep the scattered boars from rejoining the majority. The ragtag militia then sweeps in to bring down the isolated hogs. Once done, the process is repeated, and to great effect, as large numbers of the ravenous ferals are taken quickly.

Danahlia often leads the fire carriers, using Artyom's and her own spear to carry a bundle of burning hay while instructing where the others need to go based on Twinkaleni's rays of fire. Alice calls the charge for the peasants to attack once the fire wall defense is in place. Unfortunately, without the discipline of a true army, the gathered people begin to take initiative on their own, causing the process to speed up beyond the girl's control. The trio tries to keep up but things become sloppy and poorly coordinated as fire carriers drop their bundles early and improperly, too eager to join the fight, as the attack force fails to stand by until the fire wall is fully prepared. The offense becomes so out of sync that it's almost entirely destroyed when one of the few truly massive shatterheads is finally encountered.

Scattered among the horde are a handful of particularly impressive boars that tower over their lesser kin. These animals are estimated by onlookers to weigh well over five hundred pounds, some even guess that the largest are in the eight hundred range. Townsfolk and farmers alike talk of how much one such monster would fetch, not only for meat but as a fine trophy, though little is said of how the beasts could be slain.

As the rushed offense pushes toward one of the larger animals, overeager fire carriers try to split it off from the others while equally eager attackers break before the charge is called to chase after it, their minds clearly more attuned to the reward rather than the fight necessary to earn it. The fire wall is laid too far apart in their haste, leaving gaping openings to the main horde. Upon being antagonized, the monstrous creature, having ignored the slaughter of its kind until now, bellows in rage and begins to charge.

This cry causes others around it to join in, creating an oncoming tidal wave of flesh and bone. The first to try to claim the mighty beast are trampled under it and the rest flee for their lives. The peasant force crumbles and the shatterheads go on the attack.

Twinkaleni valiantly launches burst after burst of fire into the rampaging ferals, trying desperately to break their charge while shouting in between calls of "Feasta!" to have more fires started. Danahlia, Alice, and a handful of others do their best to set more bundles aflame and throw them about to ward off the attacking boars as screaming people are knocked to the ground and run over.

Twinkaleni gets the attention of the massive shatterhead and it veers off toward her with tremendous speed. Both Alice and Danahlia charge the beast from its flank intending to ram the feral in its side in the hopes that they might just be enough to knock it over or at least keep it from squishing their tiny companion. However, they both slide to a stop when Twinkaleni unleashes a wide cone of fire that washes over the entire monster. The heat taken for the spell is so great that the air around the girls chills noticeably and the flames from the burning bundles nearly die out. The enraged shatterhead squeals in pain but doesn't slow. Now cloaked in fire as its coarse hair burns, it's become a demonic war engine barreling right for the Murin mage.

Alice and Danahlia both hurl their spears, scoring hits in its thick back thigh as it passes them. Perhaps because of the wounds and maybe blinded by fire, the beast narrowly misses Twinkaleni, though it's shear mass passing so close causes her to fall over. The massive shatterhead bowls into others of its kinds, crushing some while sending others flying. The little mouse girl shakes her head in a daze and rises back to her feet, looking after the beast.

Seeing she is alright, Danahlia and Alice both chase after the massive feral as it falls to the ground, rolling in a panic or perhaps even purposely trying to put itself out. Danahalia shouts for Twinkaleni to launch her onto it as does Alice, pulling free her sword.

Focused solely on defeating the monster, Alice dashes for it with Jellybane tight in hand. She feels herself becoming lighter as Twinkaleni works her earth magic, reducing gravity's pull, and beside her Danahlia leaps. Alice follows suit, both girls getting much higher and farther than any average person would be able to manage. Flying toward the rolling boar, they both angle their weapons downward to put their full weight behind their attacks. They land on the creature's large stomach, driving their weapons deep into its chest. The effect is instant and the great beast squeals, kicking wildly, forcing the two to leave their weapons embedded in it as they leap away to safety.

Somehow, the massive creature rolls over to its feet and prepares to rise. Now unarmed, the girls back away from the monster only to have a wooden spear impale it's belly, then another, and another as furious peasants take advantage to strike at the creature while it tries to stand. Eventually, they do enough damage and the gigantic shatterhead finally stills. The charge broken, the other scattering individuals are turned away or slaughtered.

The victory is bitter sweet, as many were wounded and some even killed. Meeka's leg was broken by one of the shatterheads and has to be dragged off the field screaming in pain along with many others. As the townspeople and farmers retreat behind the safety of flaming bundles, the boars that survived the attack recongeal into the main horde. Alice and Danahlia recover their weapons and the trio falls back.

Twinkaleni is on the verge of collapse and everyone needs time to assess their wounds and catch their breath. As they rest, arguments fueled by loss and pain arise as fault is tossed around with every shouted word. Lulu, never interested in taking part in the battles, waves the girls over to her wagon where Twinkaleni is laid and promptly passes out. They explain what happened as other wagons are being filled with wounded, while still others are loaded with shatterheads to begin heading away from the pasture. As fault slowly begins turning toward a failure in planning, the girls and Lulu decide to take their leave and head back to Barley.

Chapter 6

Along the River

"But we haven't beaten the horde yet," Alice replies to Danahalia's suggestion that they end their shatterhead hunting careers.

"Who says we have to? You saw what happened today with just one of those big ones," argues Danahlia, stroking a sleeping Twinkaleni's ear in the back of Lulu's wagon.

"What about the farms and farmers? Are we just gonna let the shatterheads overrun everything?" asks Alice.

"It's not our fight. We don't owe 'em anything and if they wanna keep their land, they'll fight for it," reasons Danahlia.

Alice frowns, "But they need our help."

"And they got it. We pushed 'em back plenty, taught 'em how to beat 'em, and we even took down one of their command-boars."

"Command-boars?"

"Yeah, that's what I'm callin' the big ones."

Alice can't help but grin at that and then asks, "What do you wanna do then?"

"I don't know. I'm thinkin' we been in Barley long enough. Maybe it's time to get back on the road. See what Twi-uh, my apprentice thinks when she wakes up."

"You wanna leave?"

"Yeah. Truth is, huntin' shatterheads is more dangerous than profitable now. And with all the meat comin' in from today, those piggies are gonna be worth even less around here. I think we should head off, look for greener pastures 'n' stuff."

Alice purses her lips, "Yeah, ok. Plus if people are lookin' to blame us for what happened, we probably shouldn't stick around for that."

Danahlia nods, "Exactly."

Twinkaleni wakes after they've entered town but before they reach the Bear's Den. She calls they're interest in leaving "a prudent course," and agrees it's time to go. Once at the inn, the girls return Artyom's boar spears. The massive Urock isn't surprised that they've decided to press on, considering the low price for shatterheads now, and insists they stay one more night so they can start fresh in the morning.

As the girls are settling into bed, they discuss where they want to go next.

"Why don't we go back to the pixie forest?" Alice asks, something she had wanted to do for some time.

"You wanna go back? The pixies were wags but their kind of a long way off now don't you think?" says Danahlia, toying with the fur of one the Tokala's forearms under the sheets of their shared bed.

Twinkaleni nods up at the ceiling, "I agree, our time with the pixies was well spent, but I for one feel I've learned all I can from them."

"But they can help you learn enchanting and probably other magic too," says Alice looking to the Murin.

Twinkaleni turns to her, "I've pondered this and I feel that is not the case. Recall the trouble I had with them trying to teach me to enchant? I suspect now that this was due to a difference in the kind of energies we employ. You see, fae are far more deeply connected with the spirit world. After noticing Jellybane's extraordinary power, I theorize that this connection allows the fae to use energies from both worlds in their magic. This would make it far more potent than any mortal mage could manage, since we can only draw from our own stores and the energy found locally in our world."

"Huh, I just thought you were bad at enchanting," Danahlia grins from behind Alice's ears.

The mouse girl narrows her eyes at the Liguna, and Alice asks, "So where do you wanna go then?"

"I believe we should continue north," Twinkaleni replies.

Frowning, Alice asks, "Why do you wanna go north all the time?"

"The Gadara Mountains are the nearest border of Arsalia. The lands under them are isolated and sparsely populated. It will be a good place to disappear for a while, which I think we should. After masquerading as agents of the Order for so long, word of our presence is sure to reach them. Once it does, they may send people to investigate."

"I guess that makes sense," says Danahlia. Alice's brow furrows. She is well past being tired of worrying about the Order. Danahlia nuzzles the sensitive fluff in her ear, "Oh come on, Alice. Ya never know. We might meet some new pixies around the whatever mountains."

It tickles terribly and the Tokala can't help but giggle, her ear twitching frantically.

"Stop," she complains pushing the lizard girl away playfully and rolling to look at her. Danahlia smiles innocently and Alice concedes, "I guess we can go north, see what's up there at least."

The Liguna gives her a toothy grin and pulls her in to nuzzle her ears again.

Alice laughs, shaking her head, but then Danahlia stops, looking over her and says, "What?"

Alice rolls back to see Twinkaleni eyeing them strangely, her mouth partially opened with one brow raised.

Danahlia opens their sheets to the tiny girl, "Room for half o' one more."

"Uh... no, thank you," says Twinkaleni, rolling over.

The pair share a smile, get comfortable, and Alice blows out their candle.

The next morning, the girls bid their farewells to the Urocks, then to Lulu who is leaving Barley as well. Ferrying the girl's shatterheads, the rabbit woman has managed to make far more than she had hoped just selling her carrots and she thanks them for this. The trio then stops at the market to buy full packs worth of shatterhead meat for the road. Much of what's available is fresh or dried but some is smoked, salted, pickled, and even honeyed in an effort to preserve it and attract customers. They buy a variety of meats, their current wealth even allowing them to splurge on some honeyed shatterhead hocks. These are particularly interesting, *and* expensive, so the few they buy don't last beyond the market.

Making their way north of Barley, the girls meet a horse drawn wagon loaded with shatterheads. Several people accompany it seeking better prices for their meat elsewhere. The three are known to them and their company, as well as protection, are welcomed. The trio decides to travel with the wagon, seeing as they're going a similar direction. They discover the wagon is heading for a small fishing village some days to the northwest. The meat merchants have heard that the river running through the village has been drying out, leaving it without a source of fish. Their hope is that this will make the villagers interested in purchasing their stock of pork.

The merchants try to maintain a steady pace through the day, eager to get their unpreserved wares to their destination before they spoil. Hilly terrain and poorly maintained roads have everyone exhausted by the time they make camp late in the evening. Twinkaleni lights a fire and a shatterhead is butchered for supper. Perhaps because of fatigue or an eagerness to reach their destination, though likely both, the merchants seem agitated and the girls decide to keep to themselves.

They squabble over little things like keeping watch, how much of their own product everyone should be allowed to eat, and when they should rise in the morning. Some even argue that they shouldn't have stopped at all, reasoning that they could work in shifts, some resting while others guide the wagon, so they can get to the village

faster. This is easily beaten down by the fact that the team of two horses need to rest as well.
With all the tension, the girls wander a little ways to a mighty oak. Eating and drinking from their own stores, they discuss leaving the wagon and trying to find their own way, but not knowing the route to the village they consider staying for just a bit longer. The great tree has thick limbs and the trio decides to bed among them tonight, a decision they do not regret.

The next day, Alice is awoken by panicked cries for help. She nearly falls off her branch but manages to hold on as she looks around. The cries aren't coming from her friends, both still in the tree and waking with her, but from the meat merchants nearby. Vision blurry, she searches the ground for threats and finds a giant ant wandering around where the girls tossed their bones from last night's dinner. Alice rubs her eyes to get a better look at the creature. It's perhaps two feet in length, similar to the giant ants of the pixie forest though this one is fiery red and has stubby spikes along its back.

Alice points to it, grumbling sleepily, "Uh, ants."

"Ooo, it's a red one," says Danahlia, retrieving her spear from where she stuck it in the tree.

"Mind the stinger, they can be quite venomous," warns Twinkaleni.

"Stinger?" asks Alice, watching the insect.

"Yeah, these guys have stingers on their butts. Don't let it stick you or you'll be in a world o' hurt. Watch this," Danahlia says, leaping down with her weapon.

This alerts the ant and it turns to her. Once it finds the lizard girl, the ant rises on its four back legs, curling its abdomen under it to face forward. Its needle like stinger thrusts forth from its tapered end and a thick drop of yellowish venom appears on the tip. It waves its two front limbs in grabbing motions while keeping its mandibles wide, the stinger tipped abdomen shifting to keep Danahlia before it.

Staying well out of reach, the Liguna maneuvers around it a bit, showing how much slower it is in this attack position. The ant seems to be expecting her to come in for a frontal assault but Danahlia side steps around to its flank. It tries to keep up, awkwardly rotating in place while she taunts it, poking at it with her spear.

Twinkaleni shouts, "Feasta!" sending fire down to end the creature with a few sizzling pops.

"Hey, that was mine," the lizard girl complains up to her.

Climbing down the tree, the Murin calls back, "You're wasting time, the merchants need our help."

Danahlia frowns as Alice leaps to join her and together the girls head for the sounds of panic.

The wagon is under attack by a swarm of the venomous monsters. Several of the merchants are trying to fend them off around and atop the wagon in an attempt to save their precious cargo. They wield wooden staves and farm tools, swinging wildly at the giant insects. More than a few have been slain but with every ant felled, another three take its place. Twinkaleni begins loosing beams of fire into groups of them as Danahlia runs for the surrounded wagon. Alice hears the frightened whinny of the horses and finds them tied to a tree limb with several ants closing in. She draws her sword and races toward the equines.

On the ants' approach, the horses whine and tug at their reins, kicking blindly behind them. As one, the ants rise into their attack positions, slowly making their way toward the immobilized animals. This makes it easy for Alice, coming from behind, to slice off heads and separate thoraxes, reducing the attackers to small piles of body parts in moments.

Well versed in battling giant ants, it doesn't take long for the girls to get things under control. They defeat nearly two dozen, scouts all of them, most likely drawn to the spot by the shatterheads. One man was stung, the ants having gotten him while everyone was still sleeping, his pained cries alerting the rest. The poor old Lobovan is loaded into the wagon, his entire left arm swelling terribly. The merchants then hastily get their things together to resume their journey before more ants can arrive.

The girls decide to take a few ants for later and encourage the others to do the same, Danahlia saying the red ones have a particularly interesting flavor once the toxins are cooked and made inert. Liking the idea of having more to sell and eat, the ants are tossed into the wagon as well.

On the way, a couple of the more helpful merchants pick leaves from a particular plant and begin chewing them. Twinkaleni recognizes the plant from her book and explains how the leaves have oil that aid in pain and swelling. Those chewing occasionally spit in their palms, rubbing the extracted oil over the rabbit man's arm. The trio take up the cause too, ever eager to try new things. The leaves are remarkably bitter and have an unpleasant chalky texture that stays on the tongue even after spit out. Still, they do their part and it does seem to sooth the stung Lobovan some.

Around noon, they come to a dry river bed and the driver informs them that it's the one that travels through the fishing village they are trying to reach. The merchants are glad to see it, knowing without meat from the river's fish, the village will be eager for theirs. The road goes around some trees, taking it away from the river, and the girls decide to part ways with the wagon, instead choosing to follow the dry bed to the village. This is a great relief to Alice as the shatterheads were really starting to smell.

The river is perhaps thirty feet wide and its bed is loaded with rocks and loose silt, all parched. The plants along the shore have yet to invade it, making the girls think it hadn't been dry for too long.

Curious, Alice asks, "Why do you think the river dried up?"

"It's rained enough," comments Danahlia, picking up a small rock to hurl it at the trunk of one of the trees along the shore.

"Perhaps the problem lies at the source," suggests Twinkaleni.

Alice picks up a rock too, throwing it and hitting the same tree Danahlia did. The two quickly make a game of it, trying to best each other by hitting smaller and smaller targets. Twinkaleni eventually joins in, though she uses her magic, making several stones float about her and periodically launching one with a call of "Telefuss!"

The branch the girls are currently aiming at breaks when hit with one of the mage's stones and Danahlia mumbles, "Show off."

Twinkaleni pays it no mind and Danahlia tries to catch the next one she launches. Alice toys with the hovering rocks, giving them little pushes in different directions. As if without friction or gravity, the stones glide through the air at the fox girl's slightest touch, until they get about three feet from the mage, where they immediately fall back to the ground.

"Can you make me float too?" Alice asks hopefully.

The Murin mage gives her a side glance but then smirks. And after a few more steps, Alice can't feel the ground anymore.

"Whoa!" she barks, waving her arms and legs, trying to get some sort of traction as she slowly ascends while lazily rolling into a somersault.

It's an odd sensation to be weightless. True, Twinkaleni had used her magic to reduce gravity's effect on her before but never had she just hung in midair like this. Alice relaxes, trusting in her magically gifted friend, and begins enjoying flying in the air. Twinkaleni straightens her flight path and has her floating a few feet off the ground beside her as the Murin herself walks on.

Watching, Danahlia whines, "Hey, no fair, do me, do me!"

Twinkaleni sighs, but smiles, letting the stones fall and soon Danahlia is floating about too. The Liguna instinctively wraps her tail around Alice's ankle to steady herself, flailing just as the fox girl had. After a few moments, she relaxes and the

Murin mage has them flying in little patterns around each other.

"This is so wags!" Alice exclaims, her arms extended out to her sides as Twinkaleni sends them high enough to touch the overhanging trees' canopies.

When Danahlia passes by, she reaches out and lets her hand flow over Alice's thick full tail. The Tokala grins at her and does the same, her hand gliding over Danahlia long smooth one.

"You gotta try this, Twinkie," calls Danahlia, as she and Alice descend some.

"It does look rather enjoyable, but as the conduit for the gravitational energy, I must remain well-grounded," the Murin says while the floating girls circle her just a few feet off the ground.

Alice feels sorry for her and wonders, "Could you use wind magic to lift yourself?"

Twinkaleni ponders aloud, "Mmm, I suppose it is possible, though far too dangerous for me to put into practice. Wind is such a... free flowing element. Controlling it to the point of being able to levitate is not unheard of but would require a mastery of magic beyond me at this time."

"Other mage's can fly?" Alice asks.

"Not that I have ever seen but I have read of some who supposedly could," replies the small mouse girl.

"Must be nice," comments Danahlia, reclining in the air.

"Indeed, though as you could imagine, the Order of Thermathrogi would have little interest in-," the Murin mage stops suddenly and the girls fall to the ground.

"Ow!" Danahlia complains, rubbing an arm, "What gives?"

Alice falls on her side, painfully atop a few rocks, but isn't hurt and looks to Twinkaleni, alert. The mage is crouching and shushes the Liguna, pointing ahead along the river bed. Looking, Alice finds that there is a person laying with their back to them in some shade. After the Cold Blood bandits, the girls are made wary by this, searching and listening for signs of ambush. No immediate danger presents itself and the trio slinks off to conceal themselves in the brush along the shoreline.

Vigilant, they slowly creep along, closer to the prone figure. They stop once they can see it's a Chitali wearing a drab, brown robe. They determine the deer person to be female, lacking the antlers of her male kin. Her long, elegant neck lies still along the rocky bottom of the dry river, her face turned away from them. She has a golden coat with white spots visible along her arms and dainty, black hooves poking out from beneath her robe.

"Twinkie, toss some fire over her. If she's fakin', she'll freak for sure," whispers Danahlia.

The mouse mage nods and summons a beam of fire with a mutter of, "Feasta."

She rakes the beam well over the figure, but the Chitali doesn't react.

Danahlia purses her lips, "She's either passed out or *really* good at this."

"I'll go see. You guys stay here," says Alice, rising from their hiding spot.

"Do be careful," calls Twinkaleni from behind her.

Alice creeps closer to the female, listening, watching, and sniffing. She doesn't smell any sign of decay or notice anything else alarming. As she gets closer, she can see the Chitali is fairly young, perhaps her own age, and very slender. She has an elongated muzzle with a tiny, white furred mouth and a black nose. Her ears are leaf shaped and wide, golden on the outside but white on the inside. The girl's body is completely relaxed, her eyes closed as if in sleep. Alice sniffs a bit closer finding she smells pleasantly of fresh grass.

The fox girl places a hand on the Chitali's shoulder and gives a little shake, "Hey, are you ok?"

The deer girl's brown eyes flash open and she rasps a surprised cry making Alice jump, fur bristling. The Chitali forces a swallow and then tries to speak but only more rasps emerge from what seems a very dry throat as she weakly tries to rise.

Squatting, Alice offers one of her waterskins, "Here, drink this."

The girl immediately takes the skin and drains it. Alice smiles, watching her long, slender neck work with each swallow. The deer girl sputters and coughs a bit once she's done, but hands the skin back.

"Finally," she says, taking in a few breaths. She then says something else that Alice doesn't understand.

"What?" the fox girl replies, her head cocking to one side.

The girl repeats herself more urgently, brown eyes wide. The words are in her language but they seem so absurd Alice can't comprehend them and the girl must repeat herself several times before giving up and reaching to touch the Tokala's shoulder. The deer girl squeezes Alice gently once and then runs her long, thin fingers down her arm, over her shirt, and then her fur. Her eyes widen further as she touches the fox girl but then they grow sad.

The Chitali leans in to whisper, "Were you sent by Althea?"

Alice cocks her head to the other side, "Who?"

The Chitali smiles, though her eyes seem to get even sadder, "Oh well, thanks. You saved me. That I *am* sure of."

Alice grins and then looks over the girl, "Are you hurt? Is there anyone else out here?"

"Oh, I don't know. There might be," the girl says uncertainly, looking around.

"Were you traveling with anyone?" Alice asks.

The girl gives her narrow head a shake, "Mm, no, though Althea watches over me, most of the time."

Looking up and down the river, Alice asks, "Althea? Who's that? Is she nearby?"

"Sometimes," the girl says looking up and around, "I don't think she's here now though."

The only Althea Alice had ever heard of is the goddess, one often prayed to in times of illness. Alice had often prayed for her mother when she was ill to no avail. Though this girl can't be talking about *the* Althea, she's looking around as if expecting to see someone.

Alice looks to the Chitali, puzzled, "Ok, well, can you walk?"

The girl looks at her, perplexed, "Of course I can."

The two watch each other for a moment, Alice waiting for the girl to prove it, while the girl just looks back as if she's said something utterly ridiculous. Then the girl's gaze switches to Danahlia and Twinkaleni who join them.

Danahlia gives the girl's thigh a poke with the butt of her spear, "Hey, you a bandit?"

"Puh, of course she wouldn't admit to it," blurts Twinkaleni.

The girl looks over herself, "Nope."

"So, who are you?" Alice asks.

At this, the girl rises to her hooves and dusts herself off. Alice stands as well and the girl announces, "I'm Kaliska, Kaliska Snowtail."

Kaliska is tall, even a few inches over Danahlia, but lithe to the point of looking frail. She then does a little dance, shaking her slim hips and doing a spin as she says, "I'm an acolyte of Althea, goddess of health, taker of illness, and bringer of love."

The girls share a look and a grin, Kaliska seems unhurt and rather proud of her calling. She stares at them in turn, placing her hands on her hips with her ears perked, "Well, what are *your* names then?"

"Oh, I'm Tanya, Tanya Softpaw. This is Amber, and she's Denelia," says Alice, using their aliases while pointing to her companions in turn.

Kaliska squints at Alice, frowning, her long neck craning down to stare closely into Alice's eyes. Alice leans back under the deer girl's surprisingly intense gaze, wondering what she sees. Under the scrutiny, Alice immediately thinks she must have slipped up and somehow the girl knows she's lying about their identities.

After an uncomfortable few seconds, Kaliska snatches Alice's hands and begins fingering her palms, commenting, "You do have pretty soft paws."

Danahlia slowly lowers her spear from where she had it pointing at the girl's face the moment she moved and asks, "What were you doin' out here?"

"Sleeping," Kaliska replies simply, "I ran out of water and thought this river should have some," she then looks urgently at Alice, still holding onto the fox girl's hands, "But it didn't!"

"Oh, kay," Alice says, withdrawing her hand from the Chitali's. Kaliska looks at her with a strange pleading in her eyes as Alice pulls away. "Uh, we're headin' to a village that's supposed to be along this river. You can come along if you want."

"*That* must be where Althea wants me to go," says Kaliska, starting to walk in the wrong direction.

"Uh, it's actually this way," Alice says, hooking a thumb the way the trio had been going.

Kaliska looks back, "Are you sure?"

"Pretty sure," says Danahlia, giving Alice a questioning look.

Kaliska turns around and immediately begins marching in the other direction. The girls let her pass and then lean into each other to discuss the matter.

"This ones nuttier than a squirrel turd," asserts Danahlia.

"Perhaps dehydration and prolonged exposure to the sun has taken its toll on her mind," offers Twinkaleni, looking after the strange girl.

Watching the Chitali walk off with unknown purpose, Alice says, "She seems, nice, plus she might pass out again if she can't find water."

"Ugh, here we go," grumbles Danahlia.

"We should stick with her, at least to the village," finishes Alice.

Danahlia crosses her arms, "Now, how did I know you were gonna say that?"

Chapter 7

Snowtail

The girls catch up to the Chitali, who looks pleased they've decided to join her. Through a series of cryptic responses, and some rambling, to their questions, the trio manages to put together a spotty history of Kaliska Snowtail.

She was raised by a priest, though not her parent, in a small church devoted to the goddess Althea in a little village somewhere in the east. A healer by calling, the priest taught the young Chitali about the potential of local flora to cure various illnesses and hasten the healing of wounds. Kaliska claims to have a special gift for healing without the use of herbs or salves. Upon discovering this gift, the priest took her to travel around spreading her supposed blessing.

"You can use healing magic?" asks Alice.

"Yup... sometimes... when Althea's around... and helps me," Kaliska nods enthusiastically at first but then slower and more doubtful with every word.

Danahlia holds out a forearm with a minor scrape under it, "Can you heal this?"

Kaliska takes the offered limb and inspects it from different angles while making little uncertain noises, "Uh... mmm... ehh... hm... I don't know, Althea's not here right now to help me."

"Convenient," mumbles Twinkaleni.

"That's not convenient. Do you even know what *convenient* means?" Kaliska shoots back after giving Danahlia's booboo an experimental lick.

Twinkaleni raises a brow at this, "I do actually. Do you know what *sarcasm* means?"

Kaliska ignores her, instead rubbing her palms together vigorously, small pink tongue hanging out of the side of her mouth, with focus completely on the small patch of scratched skin on Danahlia's upraised forearm. She then extends her hands out as if to grab Danahlia's arm, but pauses an inch before actually touching the Liguna. The girls all watch expectantly but the deer girl doesn't move. Alice notices a gradual change in her eyes, a shift from focus to something more vacant.

After a strange moment, the girls look to each other, the Chitali as still as a statue. Then Danahlia looks curiously at her forearm to see that the skin has been mended and now looks as smooth and unblemished as the rest of her.

"Hey, you did it," she says happily, feeling the healed area with a clawed finger.

Kaliska still doesn't move.

Danahlia waves a hand before her eyes getting no reaction at all, "Uh, Kaliska?"

The girls look closely at her for a time. She doesn't breathe or even blink. Alice blows on her face and ears while the others poke at her a bit, trying to illicit some sort of response.

"Ticks, are you dead?" asks Danahlia.

Twinkaleni pokes around at her legs, "Ye-,um, it doesn't seem, likely, but the complexity of healing magic does strain the body, and she was already rather weak. Perhaps it-"

Danahlia is sending a probing claw toward one of Kaliska's eyeballs when the deer girl takes a sudden inhale, making the girls jump, "Oh, hey, did it work?"

Danahlia looks curiously at her, holding up her forearm for inspection, "Uh, yeah. You ok?"

"Yay!" Kaliska cheers, doing her little dance again before starting back off down the river.

"What happened to you? After you healed Da- uh, Denelia?" wonders Alice, following after her.

"Happened? When? Who?" Kaliska asks, genuinely puzzled.

"Me. You healed me and then froze for like *two* minutes," says Danahlia coming up to the deer girl's other side.

"Are you sure?" asks Kaliska.

"Uh, yeah, we *all* saw it," assures Danahlia, the others nodding.

"You guys are weird, I like you," says the Chitali, apparently dismissing the entire incident.

The girl's follow after her and get a few more precious details about the unusual girl. Once the war began, the priest left Kaliska back at his church so he could tend to the wounded soldiers closer to the front line. After a time, Kaliska claims that the goddess, Althea, began to visit and told her to begin her travels again so she could share her blessed healing with others.

"But she keeps leaving. Then I end up alone in the middle of nowhere. That's rude, right? It's like, she bugs and bugs to go out and spread her love and cheese, so I finally do, and then she just leaves, like I'm supposed to know where I'm going," Kaliska says, looking about as if intending to spot the divine being among the bushes at any time.

"You can hear and speak to this goddess?" asks Twinkaleni, skeptically.

Kaliska looks down at the smaller girl, "No, I just said, she left. I don't know where she is. Maybe to that village you guys are goin' to, to find water. We need water."

"What does she look like?" Alice asks.

"Oh, I don't know, I only hear her sometimes. She sounds pretty though, and purple," replies Kaliska.

From behind her, Danahlia twirls a finger beside her head.

"I'm not crazy!" Kaliska exclaims without looking, and then sorrowfully insist, "I'm not."

Alice walks a little closer to the distraught girl, "I don't think you're crazy."

"You look around as if expecting to see your goddess, though you yourself say you've never seen her," comments Twinkaleni.

Looking at the ground before her, Kaliska sniffs, tears welling in her eyes, "Because sometimes she sounds really close and I might see her but she's always hiding, and now I can't find her and I don't know what I'm supposed to do."

Alice places an arm around the Chitali as they walk, "You should come with us, at least to the village. Like you said, she might be there waitin'."

Kaliska sniffs, smiling a little at the Tokala's offer, "Ok."

They travel well into the afternoon until they find a nice big oak they feel will carry their weight. After the encounter with red ants and seeing what they can do with just one sting, they don't want to take any chances in this area. Twinkaleni wants them to use what's left of their energy and the daylight to get in some sparring. The girls, all tired, grudgingly agree to it.

The tiny Murin has gotten significantly better at using her sticks, one short and one longer to represent her rapier and main gauche. This is greatly imparted to Alice and Danahlia encouraging her to use magic to aid her as well. While sparring, she now uses little bursts of wind to make the larger girls blink or look away, letting her dart in for a strike. She's also become adept at using her earth magic to forcibly alter the girl's positions and stances to create the same result. Alice and Danahlia sometimes find their feet sliding away, unable to touch the ground, or their entire bodies being levitated and turned so the tiny Murin can close for an attack. Her earth magic is slower to summon than the little puffs of air, leaving her open as well, but she is definitely getting better and is very proud of it.

Kaliska watches in amazement as they have their little mock battles. She immediately wants to join in too, but it becomes clear she has no practice in combat. Still, the Chitali is quick to take advantage of her long limbed body to outreach the others when given the chance. They have fun for a time and all become even more exhausted once evening comes. Settling down for supper, they offer Kaliska some shatterhead meat, but the deer girl looks at it in disgust before gathering up some grasses and leaves, munching on these instead.

As the girls make their way up the tree for the night, they notice Kaliska's dainty hooves and clawless fingers don't allow her to make much progress. Twinkaleni solves this by using her earth magic to levitate the girl and Alice guides her to a branch. The deer girl grips her branch tight with both arms and legs, but seems to enjoy her new vantage point. She asks about the trio and they give her their practiced backstories.

All where orphans left to the Order of Thermathrogi and trained for the roles they currently play. Alice was trained in various weapons and combat techniques for her role as a guard. Twinkaleni, with her magical talent, was of course taught to harness it so that she may one day serve as a full battle mage for the Arsalian army. Danahlia is Twinkaleni's handler and caretaker, meant to guide her as she gains first hand field experience.

Kaliska's ability to pay attention varies greatly. Sometimes she listens enraptured, while other times she interrupts with completely irrelevant questions. For example, when Alice was describing her supposed archery training, the Chitali asks what kind of food she was eating then. Still, something about the girl has Alice drawn to her. The fox ponders this while Twinkaleni lengthily explains something about magic and how it drains the body when Kaliska's previous freezing episode comes up. In the middle of her explanation, Kaliska begins what might be a prayer.

"...and Tanya, who is nice. Oh and Amber, watch over her too when you get back, though you don't need to as much because she has magic and large eyes," the Chitali says into her palms, held together before her nose.

She then raises her hands and opens them as one might if they were releasing a captured bird. She even watches for a few seconds as if the wind is carrying her words away before turning to the others to say, "Hope those get to her."

The trio shares a confounded look, one of many today, before saying their goodnights and going to sleep.

Well before dawn, Alice is awoken by something tickling her feet. She shifts and kicks, bleary vision revealing Kaliska to be the culprit. The deer girl, having gotten from her own branch to Alice's, now sits near the base with her legs dangling on either side of it, leaning over and touching the padded bottoms of Alice's feet.

Alice kicks some more, giggling, "What're you doing?"

Kaliska grins, gliding her fingers over and between the fox's soft pads and toes, "Good, you're awake. Its morning, we should go. I don't want to miss Althea if she's at that village."

Alice groans, looking around to see that the sun isn't even out yet, "It's too early, we'll go in an hour or so."

Kaliska frowns, tickling Alice's feet more vigorously, "But I need to pee and I can't get down."

Alice kicks some more and groans again. She helps the deer girl down, holding her hands while Kaliska hangs off the branch so she can fall safely the rest of the way. Kaliska runs off the moment she's down and Alice lies back on her branch, but it's too late, she's awake and a new day has begun.

The others wake a little after and they all climb down for breakfast.

"Where's Kali?" asks Danahlia, picking out some shatterhead meat from her pack.

Alice looks around frowning, "She needed to go to the bathroom, but that was a while ago now."

"I don't like this. We should move on quickly. If she was some sort of spy, she may be leading bandits to us as we speak," warns Twinkaleni, twitching her nose and whiskers.

"Come on, she's a little strange, but I don't think she's a bad person," says Alice, a knot of worry tightening in her gut.

"A *little* strange?" Danahlia exclaims before stripping a rib.

"Ok, maybe a lot strange, but she heals people. How could she be bad?" asks Alice, retrieving her own breakfast as they prepare to leave.

Nibbling a bit of meat, Twinkaleni says, "Consider she has very few supplies, only a single water skin and no weapon. How would she survive out here unless she had support nearby?"

"Just lucky I guess," comes Kaliska's voice, the girl walking up to them from behind a tree, something in her clasped hands.

"Hey, where did you go?" asks Alice, Danahlia and Twinkaleni reaching for their weapons.

The Chitali freezes under the three's glares, "What?"

"Where did you go?" Alice asks again more sternly, taking a step closer.

Kaliska backpedals, her ears drooping as she points, "I... over there, behind the bushes. Did you step in it? I'm sorry, I didn't mean to go so close to the tree, I just, I couldn't hold it anymore."

"No, where did you go after? Al-Tanya says you were gone for a while," says Danahlia, pointing her spear with one hand at the girl.

Kaliska attempts to step away again but trips over a surface root. As she tries to catch herself, her hands come apart, revealing a handful of blueberries that then tumble about her. She falls without grace onto her bottom with a little "Oh," and then tries to slide back on her hands and hooves talking frantically, her eyes locked onto the spear point, "I'm sorry, I thought I heard Althea and I went to look for her, but she ran away again, and then I found a berry bush. I was so hungry, I...I ate, most of them, but I brought some. I'm sorry."

A wave of shame washes over Alice, heavy enough to make her shoulders sag. She immediately drops to the girl's side and it physically hurts to see the frightened Chitali flinch at her offered hand, "No, we're sorry. We thought you might be sneakin' off to get bandits to attack us or something. We're sorry, right?" She says the last looking to the others.

Danahlia lowers her spear, guilt evident in her expression, "Yeah, we're sorry. We just had some nasty encounters before. I guess we're a little edgy."

Twinkaleni says nothing, still looking at the girl suspiciously. As Alice and Danahlia help gather the blueberries, the Murin mage asks, "So you heard your goddess, Althea, and went looking for her?"

Slowly relaxing, Kaliska replies, looking around at her dropped berries, "I thought I did. I don't know if it was, I get confused. She whispers sometimes and other times she yells from far away, so I can't hear what she's saying very well."

"I see," says Twinkaleni crossing her arms, "And does Althea ever tell you to do things?"

Kaliska looks to her, not needing to look up despite being seated, and frowns, "She told me to help people and go places, or at least, directions."

"And has she ever told you to harm anyone?" asks Twinkaleni.

Alice glares at the mage, "Amber, stop it."

Kaliska scowls, clearly getting upset, "No! Althea's a good goddess! She wants me to help spread her blessing!"

"One more question if you will indulge me," presses Twinkaleni, "Has she ever referred to herself *as* the goddess, Althea?"

This only angers the Chitali even more and she grimace's darkly at the Murin, huffing breathes from between clenched teeth. But then her expression drops to a deep frown as she rises and dusts herself off. With a last sharp glance to the small mage, Kaliska grumbles, in an almost childlike manner,

"You're not very nice," and then heads back toward the dry river. Before she gets more than a few steps, she spins and asks Alice, "Hey, can I have some more water?"

Alice offers her a waterskin and they walk on together, Danahlia and Twinkaleni following. The party travels along the shore when they can and hop back into the bed when the density of trees and bushes force them. Alice recounts their adventures in Barley, saving Lulu, their subsequent battles with the shatterheads, the Urocks of the Bear's Den, and the encounters with thieves and bandits. In turn, Kaliska offers a bit more of her own story, how she had been traveling to just a few places near her small church that she remembered from her travels with the priest, but was constantly nagged by Althea to go further. This was her first attempt to do so.

Her actual story is rather short but she tends to be sidetracked easily and rambles on about minute details. Kaliska also randomly interrupts herself and others to point out plants along the way, revealing a knowledge of them that impresses even Twinkaleni. She collects some that she thinks will be useful, or edible. She crams them into her robe, pockets, sleeves, anywhere, and more than a few fall out as she walks.

She can identify almost every type of plant and tells the girls if they're edible or if they can be used in medicine. Some can but only if certain things are done to prepare them. One needs to be chewed into pulp that can then be lathered onto wounds to aid in pain, swelling, and healing. Another needs to be made into a fine paste but is good for warts, while another can be combined with many others to amplify their effects. A few more, she just stuffs into her mouth.

The girls walk for much of this day as well, but with all there is to talk about, the time passes quickly. Late in the afternoon, Twinkaleni proposes a race to the top of a small hill and another particularly large tree. Kaliska starts off without anyone calling for it and everyone sprints after her. Long, slender legs carry the deer girl with amazing speed as she bounds more than runs. Alice and Danahlia are hard pressed to keep up, while they all leave Twinkaleni in the dust. But the Murin mage has a new trick up her sleeve.

She calls, "Vespis Fleda!" attracting Alice's attention. The fox girl looks back to see Twinkaleni waving her short arms around in wide circles as a strange wind begins to pick up from behind them. Alice watches in amazement as the wind strengthens, becoming a constant current blowing hard enough to make Twinkaleni's loose clothes drift forward despite her running in the same direction. The clever Murin uses the wind as a boost, her short legs carrying her with ever increasing speed. As she catches up to the others, Alice can feel the strength of the magic infused wind growing stronger and stronger until she's running with it at her back as well. With the powerful gust pushing her on, her steps become lighter and quicker.

Alice laughs out loud at the simple pleasure of running as fast as she can. Aided by the wind, she feels exhilarated and free even as her legs tire and lungs burn. Danahlia whoops with joy, her long tail and cloak waving wildly after her as Kaliska bounds higher into the air, her arms out to her sides as if intending to take flight. Then the wind suddenly stops and Alice looks back to find Twinkaleni on the ground. They all rush to her, Alice and Danahlia kneeling by her side while Kaliska looks on from a few feet away.

The small Murin rolls herself over onto her side with a hiss. Her tiny pink fingers are inflamed with small scratches and one pant leg is torn, revealing a nasty scrape along her knee and shin, the light gray fur there darkening with fresh blood.

Danahlia helps her sit up, huffing, "What happened?"

"Oh, that looks painful," says Alice, using the fur of one forearm to clean away bits of grit on the small girl's palms.

"I'm… ok. I'm ok. Really. I just lost, my balance," assures Twinkaleni, breathing hard and waving them away. She then lets out a little, "Oh," at seeing her torn pants and bleeding leg.

Alice turns to Kaliska, "Can you heal her?"

Kaliska steps closer but the mouse girl exclaims, "No! No, that's quite alright. It's just a minor scratch."

"But it's bleedin'," says Alice.

"It's alright. Kali's healing magic doesn't hurt at all," assures Danahlia.

"Ok," Kaliska announces, taking a deep breath while snapping her fingers twice, then clapping her hands twice, before rigorously rubbing them together.

Twinkaleni moans "No," scooting away.

Danahlia stops her, "Let her do it."

Alice moves out of the way as Kaliska kneels before the little mouse girl. Kaliska continues rubbing her hands together but lifts them over her head as she leans in to examine Twinkaleni's leg. The Chitali gets close enough to lick it, but doesn't this time, instead staring intently at the wound. The others, including Twinkaleni lean in too, curious as to what she is looking so closely for, but they jump back as Kaliska instead suddenly snatches both of the Murin's hands. Twinkaleni tries to pull away but with a dead stare, Kaliska keeps them held, her thumbs rubbing over the much smaller girl's palms.

After a few yanks by the Murin, Kaliska lets them go to pull up the mouse mage's pant leg. Twinkaleni looks at her palms to find them healed, perfectly pink as they usually are.

"Ooo, you're soft," Kaliska mentions, rubbing the fine, light gray fur along Twinkaleni's leg, though she stays away from the wound.

The Murin mage endures this for a time until Kaliska begins rubbing her muzzle pleasurably along her leg.

"*That* I believe will do," Twinkaleni grumbles, pushing the deer girl's face away.

Kaliska grins and licks her thumb. She rubs it over the wound to wipe away the blood. Twinkaleni flinches but then stares. The scrape is gone. She's missing a ragged line of fur, but her skin is completely healed.

The Murin tentatively feels around the area with a finger, then with her whole hand, "Impressive."

"How's it feel?" Danahlia asks.

"As if it was never injured at all," replies Twinkaleni smiling up at the Chitali.

Alice grins at the deer girl too, "That was amazing, Kali."

Kaliska does a little dance, bobbing her fists before her chest as she stands, "Yup, yup, yup yup yup."

Danahlia helps Twinkaleni to her feet while planting a little kissing atop her forehead. The Murin waves her off, and they begin walking on toward the hill. Alice and Danahlia watch her intently for a few steps but the mouse mage seems perfectly fine. Kaliska bounds up the hill energetically but then collapses. Sharing a look, the three race up after her to find the Chitali prone on her belly, a hand over her eyes to shield them from the setting sun. She points without a word into the distance.

Following her finger and raising a hand over her own eyes, Alice spots a village along the dry river. It's still a ways off, but at least they could see it now. "That must be it," she says.

Beyond the village, the terrain seems to get rougher, leading into a particularly imposing mountain tall enough to have a white peak and wide enough to keep them from seeing beyond.

Alice points to it, "Is that the border of Arsalia?"

"I don't believe so. We've come a ways but I was under the impression that it was still quite a distance off," replies Twinkaleni.

"We're catching up to Althea," Kaliska says happily, rolling around in the grass.

Danahlia tosses off her backpack and cloak to plop down beside the Chitali, "Yep. Hope that village has a well or somethin'. I'm runnin' low on water."

It's impossible to tell from here, but Alice hopes so too. With four drinking from their limited supply, the party is going to need a refill soon.

Dusk now, the girls settle down for dinner and discuss how wags Twinkaleni's new spell is. The Murin takes the complements, admitting that it was meant to boost her own speed, but is glad it turned out to be of some use to everyone. She quickly turns the conversation toward Kaliska's magic, very interested to know how it works. But the mage is quickly frustrated by the Chitali's vague responses. From what little Alice can grasp, it seems both use an inherent energy from within, but Twinkaleni typically only uses this energy to gather and alter more energy from the environment while Kaliska claims her goddess aids her when healing. Twinkaleni wants to know a tangible local source for this "divine" energy, which she says must be considerable for healing, but Kaliska insists it's in some way imparted to her by, the currently absent, Althea.

"And where is she?" demands Twinkaleni, standing over the deer girl, who is lying in the grass on her back, "She must be nearby for you to draw on such power."

"I don't know," Kaliska replies, saying her words slowly, "I *thought* that's why we were going to the village, to find her."

"But you healed without her presence. How could you have harnessed her energy from such a great distance, and without even knowing if she is there or not? It doesn't make sense!" argues Twinkaleni, her tiny hands giving animation to her frustration.

"Althea is a goddess," Kaliska says, spreading her arms wide to the sky. "She helps me," the deer girl points to herself, speaking and gesturing as if trying to convey something to someone of very limited intelligence.

The little mouse girl throws up her arms and makes an irritated squeak before turning and marching away. Danahlia and Alice have stayed out of it though the Murin seeks the Liguna's counsel now. She talks so rapidly and with such irritation that it comes out more like one long sound rather than actual words.

Kaliska rolls closer to where Alice is sitting, looks up at her and asks, "Geez, what is she not getting?"

Alice just grins and shrugs. When the Chitali rolled, Alice notices a generous portion of one long leg is left showing, leading Alice to suspect that the deer girl isn't wearing anything under her robe. She gives Kaliska a questioning look, but only gets an innocent smile in return.

The tree atop the hill is secluded enough that the girls decide to sleep on the ground tonight. The tall grass is soft and dry, making for a decent place to lie down. Before bed, Kaliska makes another one of her strange prayers, releasing it into the wind just as she had done before. Considering the deer girl's apparent favor from her goddess, Alice wonders if *she* was the one who had been praying wrong all along.

She asks about this and Kaliska replies, "It doesn't matter how you pray. It's who's in your heart when you do that matters."

Chapter 8

Fiske and the Great Horn

The next morning, Kaliska wakes Alice again, this time by smelling about her ears. The Tokala's sleepy eyes reveal the Chitali's narrow face right beside her, sniffing curiously. Alice is about to ask what she's doing when Kaliska licks the inside of one.

"Wuahh!" Alice shudders at the strange sensation.

"Oh good, you're awake. Look, Look!" Kaliska points excitedly.

Sticking a finger in her now moist ear, Alice follows the deer girl's gesture to a small herd of horses grazing in the meadow to the northwest of their hill. There are at least sixteen individuals, three foals and the rest look to be adults. Alice had only seen a few horses and those were ridden or otherwise owned. She doesn't see anyone accompanying them which leads her to believe that these are wild. Kaliska watches them, sitting up with her hands clasped to her chest, a pleased smile on her face. Alice sees the others are still asleep so she props herself on her elbows to join in watching the ferals. The adults mostly graze, though some wander around as if patrolling for danger. The younger ones run about under the watchful gazes of their mothers, rearing challenges to anyone who pays them any mind.

After a few minutes, Danahlia stretches, spotting them too, "Must be gettin' close to the middle o' nowhere."

"Not nowhere, Fiske," corrects Kaliska.

The Liguna pauses mid-stretch, "What?"

Kaliska points to the village, "We're getting close to Fiske."

"That's the village along the river? You've been there?" asks Alice.

"Yeah, I think so, a while ago, once," the deer girl replies, her voice doing that thing where she loses certainty with each word.

"Remember anythin' about it?" Danahlia asks, raising a brow to her.

"Yeah, something about it being haunted," Kaliska says, nonchalantly.

Alice turns away from the horses to blurt, "It's haunted?"

"Ooor, something..." Kaliska trails off, her head cocked to one side as she tries to recall.

Once Twinkaleni wakes, they have breakfast and head toward the village. The Murin calls Fiske's possible haunting "nonsense," and then goes on in length about the impossibility of ghosts.

Danahlia counters, "My mom saw a ghost once." This earns her the attention of the others and she grins, "She told me she saw it when she wasn't far outta hatchling."

"Where?" Twinkaleni asks skeptically.

"It was in the mountains, waaaay west o' here," says Danahlia, pointing with her spear, "See, the tribe was headin' to its winter camp grounds, but winter was comin' early that year and they were runnin' outta time. They generally went around, but with the weather changin' so fast, they had to try a faster, more dangerous route between two mountains."

Kaliska bobs up and down impatiently, "When's the ghost coming?"

"Well," Danahlia continues, "The route was dangerous because the snow on those mountains was known to cause avalanches. Mom's tribe tried to get through quick but a freak blizzard forced'em to hunker down right at the most dangerous part. That night, as everyone was huddlin' together in their stickups around tiny fires strugglin' just to keep warm against the frigid winds, an avalanche came and buried 'em all. For two days they were buried until mom's family managed to dig out, only to find they were the only ones who did."

"Everyone else died?" Alice asks.

"No, they were just the first ones to dig their way out. Mom was a great digger, I got her claws," Danahlia replies, wiggling her fingers. "So as they spread out to help rescue the other families, mom dove back into the snow to try to find her friend's stickup. It was buried the deepest and took hours to find it. When she finally tunneled deep enough, there it was, frozen solid. Mom thought the worst, but she could hear her friend's voice comin' from inside. She wore her claws to the nubs rippin' through ice and frozen hides but finally made it in. There in the middle of the stickup was her friend,

Tahki, all white and blue where she used to be tan and brown, tryin' desperately to get a fire goin'. Scraping her flint and tinder together, she kept cryin', 'It won't light, it won't light!' Mom turns to scream for help up the tunnel she dug, but when she looks back to Tahki, she was gone. All they found was the little bundle of twigs that refused to light."

"Oh, that's sad," says Kaliska.

"Preposterous," claims Twinkaleni, hiking up her backpack, "If they had been frozen, Tahki's family's bodies would have been found."

"They were found. Right, over, HERE!" shouts Danahlia, jumping at the Murin with both claws raised. Twinkaleni lets out a startled squeak and nearly falls backward, much to the amusement of the others. The girls continue to travel along the dry river, telling ghost stories to pass the time.

As they near the village they think is Fiske, the party sees the place looks like any other. A huddle of small, unimpressive houses made from what can be found locally, mostly lumber with grass thatched roofs but also hills that have been dug into and hollowed out. These tend to be smaller than the houses and judging by the doors, are likely to homes of the more diminutive residence.

Alice notices Danahlia crouched down as Twinkaleni whispers something into her ear. The Liguna nods and exchanges a few waterskins with the Murin. She then tells the girls that she's going to scout ahead and that they'll meet along the river on the other side of the village. Before Alice can question this, Danahlia breaks from the group and runs off toward some thicker brush.

Alice looks to Twinkaleni and the Murin gives her head a little shake, raising a brow at Kaliska. Alice takes this to mean she doesn't want anything said before the deer girl. The Chitali herself obliviously munches on leaves she pulls from bushes they pass. After a time, Twinkaleni sidles up to Alice and puts a hand on her leg to slow her pace, letting Kaliska get a few steps ahead of them. The Murin then motions for Alice to lend an ear.

"I think it wise if Danny is not seen in Fiske. Anyone tracking us will no doubt be looking for a Liguna in a red cloak, but we should not raise suspicion, especially now that we've acquired Kali," she whispers.

Alice nods her understanding and the trio makes their way into the village.

They get more than a few looks, though most simply go about their business. Alice feels tension in the air, like a mix of anxiety, fear, and uncertainty, lingering over the place. Twinkaleni seems to feel it too, the Murin walking closer to Alice while shifting her gaze about at every movement. Kaliska, by contrast, strides on happily, peering about as if the village is a newly discovered world of wonders.

The deer girl stops suddenly, her ears perking up, making the others pause as well.

"Althea?" she calls, looking around and then starts on again, her large teardrop shaped ears angling as if trying to pick up some faint sound. Her pace quickens, Alice and Twinkaleni needing to jog to keep up, as the Chitali calls again, "Althea?! Where are you?"

Twinkaleni is falling behind and tugs on Alice's tail to get her to slow. They're drawing a lot more attention now and the Murin advises they not associate themselves too much with Kaliska. The two fallback some but keep the deer girl in their sights.

She eventually stops at a small dwelling that is little more than two angled walls made of sticks and grass that meet a few feet over the ground like a roof without a house under it.

There's a short Leeseran sitting in front of it trying to weave what might be some sort of fish trap or basket. There are several more in various states of completion around him. The girls keep their distance and watch as Kaliska approaches the squirrel man. He spots her shadow and looks up to her, revealing one of his ears had been cut, leaving it in two ragged pieces. A scar leading from the damaged ear travels down his face and over one cheek, having claimed his left eye.

Kaliska leans in and says something Alice can't hear. The squirrel man stares at her in the most peculiar manner and then dismisses her to continue his work. The Chitali circles his house, clearly searching for something, while the man resumes his weaving. Curiously waiting, Alice notices he favors only one hand, the other simply placed to prop up his craft. Peering closer, Alice sees it's because his left hand has been badly burned, the flesh of several furless, waxy looking fingers having been stiffly fused together by some long past encounter with fire.

After Kaliska rings the Leeseran's dwelling three times, the man says something, becoming agitated by the girl's presence. Only then does she seem to find what she's looking for in the man's damaged hand. A sudden jubilance takes her as she places her own hands around the burnt appendage. The man is taken off guard and doesn't look to know what to do. Kaliska begins rubbing his hand between hers in tight circles. The man tries to pull away at first but after a few seconds, looks to his damaged appendage in wide eyed wonder. A few other people passing by stop to stare at the commotion as Kaliska raises the man's hand, rubbing his fingers vigorously with her own.

After nearly two minutes of this, the healer focuses on his index and middle fingers, rubbing while steadily pulling at them. It's a slow process but eventually the once fused fingers split. As Kaliska moves on to the fusion of his middle and ring fingers, the man curls his freed finger experimentally, his mouth dropping open. Kaliska works until all five fingers are once more independent and able to move freely.

By the time she's done, a small crowd has gathered and murmurs excitedly as the man examines his restored hand in undisguised astonishment. Some give thanks to Kaliska as well as to various gods, including Althea. The deer girl grins widely at the man for a moment before toppling over. The Leeseran catches her and demands water be brought immediately. Several people dart off in different directions, pushing past Alice and Twinkaleni.

A few with pitchers and gourds dash together in the same direction. Figuring they may be going to a water source, Alice takes Twinkaleni's waterskins and the ones the mage was holding for Danahlia, telling her to watch over Kaliska while she runs off after them. Some distance away, they lead her to a well with a considerable line. The dashers, all youths, line up at the back, talking excitedly of what they just witnessed. Alice joins them and asks about the line for water. However, they're far too interested in their own conversation to bother responding or even looking back at her. She tries again and they purposely turn away to shut her out.

Getting frustrated, she's about to shout but a girl's voice from behind says, "The river's dry, didn't you see it?"

Alice turns to a young Lutarin girl behind her, holding a large clay pitcher to her chest. The otter girl is brown furred, like most of her kind, and looks up at the Tokala with large, black eyes.

"Uh, yeah, I saw. Do you know why it's dried up?" Alice asks.

The younger girl shakes her head, "No, nobody does. But they've been rationing the water in the well ever since."

Alice looks ahead at the well to where a few people are carefully filling everyone's containers with ladles, "Hasn't anyone gone to check the source?"

When the otter girl doesn't reply, Alice looks to her.

Wide eyed, the younger girl asks, "Don't you know? The source is in the Great Horn, and that mountain's haunted."

Alice raises a brow, "I've heard the same thing about this village."

The girl shakes her head again, "No, it's the mountain. No one goes up there."

"What's it haunted with?" Alice wonders, looking over the village to the massive ridge.

"Monsters. I've heard that if you're near the Great Horn, especially at night, you can see their glowing, blue eyes watching you. If you ever see those eyes, you need to run, or you'll get eaten. No one's supposed to go near the Great Horn," says the young Lutarin.

Perhaps all the time spent with Twinkaleni has made Alice skeptical, because in her mind she immediately tries to come up with practical reasons to disprove the haunted mountain story. But the girl goes on with things people have said about it, most of them involving imaginative creatures and even hostile plants that guard the forest surrounding the peek. The time in the line passes fairly quickly with all the girl has to say about the mountain that overlooks her village and soon Alice is up to get her waterskins filled.

A Lotarin woman with a ladle, part of a team of three, looks at all of Alice's waterskins, "I can fill three of those, but anymore will be a brin each. Either that or you'll have to come back tomorrow."

Alice frowns, having never needed to pay for water before, and digs around in her purse pocket. The raccoon woman looks surprised when she's handed a shil, which is enough to fill all her skins and the otter girl's pitcher all the way up. The

Lutarin thanks Alice before wandering away, wobbling under the weight of her filled pitcher. Before she gets too far, Alice calls to her and asks if there's a trade post or general store around. The girl tries to point but nearly loses her hold on her pitcher and has Alice follow her back home.

She doesn't live terribly far away and after delivering the water to her grateful mother, the otter girl leads Alice to a small shop. She leaves her then, the girl's mother having told her to come right back after showing Alice where it was. Noting the location, Alice backtracks and finds Twinkaleni searching for her near the well.

"What happened to Kaliska?" Alice asks, looking around.

"She will be just fine. The people here are treating her like some sort of saint," Twinkaleni says dourly.

"You think we should leave her here?"

"I believe that would be the best course. She draws far too much attention to herself, and it would be wise for us to keep a low profile for now."

Alice grudgingly agrees, not particularly wanting to leave her new friend. She then leads Twinkaleni to the small shop so they can resupply. It doesn't have much but they do manage to procure some salted fish, preserved before the river dried. It smells a little funny and is well overpriced, so they only buy a little. Back on the street, the girls head north to meet up with Danahlia. Just as they're about to leave the village, Kaliska calls them from behind.

The deer girl races toward them at a full bound, shouting, "Hey!" When she reaches them she huffs, "Where, are you going?"

Alice points to the mountain, "Plan was to find a way through that. Aren't you gonna stay here?"

"Wuh, uh, well, not if you're not going to," replies Kaliska.

"But what about finding Althea?" Alice asks.

"She said you were leaving and that I should go with you. She's pretty sure you're gonna need my help," Kaliska assures them.

"The people here certainly appreciate your aid. Perhaps you should stay and heal a few more villagers," suggests Twinkaleni.

Kaliska looks bewildered at the Murin, "Althea said I need to go with you! She said I'd help the village more if I did, so that's what I'm gonna do." She marches off past them and then looks over her shoulder, "Well, we goin' or not?"

Alice grins, happy to have the unusual girl back, "Yeah, but first we need to get you some adventurin' stuff."

Back at the store, they buy Kaliska some more waterskins and a large woven basket that can be worn sort of like a backpack. The small trading post doesn't have much of a selection but they decide to get a large, thick, beige tarp that they might want to sleep on or use as a blanket in case it gets cold in the mountain. Kaliska carries this proudly in her new back-sket and the girls fill their skins at the well before heading off to look for Danahlia.

Following along the dried river, they head northeast for a time, the Great Horn looming ever closer. It's clear not many people, if any, come this way. The land here is rough and unkempt, without even footpaths cutting through the thickening foliage. The base of the mountain is a dense forest. Once within, the cry and rustle of unseen birds and beasts sound from all about them. Alice's ears angle at each unfamiliar call, though none seem threatening. She decides to tell the others of what the otter girl said about the mountain being haunted.

"Oh yeah, now I remember. Fiske isn't the one that's haunted, it's the mountain," Kaliska says happily, then adds in a spooky voice while fluttering her fingers at her companions, "They say anyone who tries to climb it, never returns. Or they don't get very far before returning, because it's haunted."

"You are aware we are heading to this supposed haunted mountain?" asks Twinkaleni.

Kaliska says cheerily, "Don't worry, we'll be ok."

The Murin cocks an eyebrow at her, "Did Althea tell you this?"

"Uh-huh. She also said we should watch our eyes," Kaliska replies, trying to cross hers.

"Riiight, our eyes," Twinkaleni says skeptically.

As Alice goes on about the strange things she's heard of the creatures that dwell in the Great Horn's forest, a sharp wind blows over one of her ears. She half ducks and turns to look behind her, one hand on her sword handle, but sees nothing. Then movement to her right reveals Danahlia beside her, grinning.

"Danny!" she exclaims, but then corrects herself, "I mean, Denelia."

"Hey, Kali came too?" asks the Liguna.

"Yup yup, and you guys can drop the act, I know you're not who you say you are, especially you," Kaliska says, waggling a finger at Danahlia.

Twinkaleni looks in shock to the deer girl, "How could you possibly-"

Alice blurts, "Wuh, what do you mean? Of course we are. Who else could we be?"

Kaliska waggles her hips as she replies, "I, don't, know, but Althea said you weren't. She said you had good hearts though so it's wags."

The trio pauses and looks to each other as Kaliska walks on.

"What do you guys think?" whispers Alice.

Danahlia peers over at the Chitali, "I'm kinda startin' to think Deer Nuts might actually have a goddess somewhere."

"Nonsense," claims Twinkaleni in a hushed tone, "We've seen no evidence of such a being."

"But what about her healing, and how did she know about us?" asks Alice.

"Healing is a very rare talent, but it isn't unheard of. It's magic, just as mine is. And as for her supposed divine information, she could simply be guessing. We *are* strangers to this land. Many who choose to wander the roads do so with little interest in leaving word of their passing. We are hardly the first to create alternate identities," insists Twinkaleni, though she sounds as if trying to convince herself as well as her companions.

Danahlia grins as they move on, "She's with us now, probably not a bad idea to have a healer on the team, even if she hears things."

"Yeah," Alice smiles back and then calls, "Hey Kali! Don't you wanna know who we really are?"

Kaliska looks back at them, surprised, "Uh, yeah, ok."

So the girls introduce themselves. They tell the Chitali how they met one another and of the adventures they've had. They tell her stories of fighting jellies and befriending pixies. They even tell her about the swamp with the giant toads and mosquitoes, the forest children, and their battle with the agent from the Order. Kaliska is amazed with their tales and agrees that their real stories were much more interesting than their made up ones.

The party of four follows the dried river, knowing they will need to refill their water supply eventually. Currently, the source of the river is their only lead but the dense forest around them is proof that there is water here, somewhere. As they go on with their stories, Alice notices its getting steadily darker the deeper into the mountain they go. It's getting late in the day, but the darkness is mostly attributed to the dense forest canopy overhead. Danahlia suggests they scout the area before picking a spot for the night.

They split into two groups, Alice and Kaliska going off together.

Looking around, Alice finds that though numerous and tall, the trees here aren't particularly thick, which means it's likely they'll have to sleep on the ground. Kaliska wanders from plant to plant, picking leaves and carelessly tossing them into the basket on her back. Not all or even most make it in, but she doesn't seem to mind in the least. Alice hears the rustle of fleeing creatures and occasionally sees the shifting of leaves or branches in their wake but nothing dangerous appears.

Looking over to where Kaliska is stooped to gather more leaves, Alice runs into a spider web. It isn't an imposing obstacle but as always, plenty icky. As she's pulling the nearly invisible strands from her ears, Kaliska makes a startled noise, standing straight up.

"What?" Alice asks, gingerly plucking more web from about her head.

Kaliska bounds over to her and points, "That malabi sapling just hit me."

Alice pauses, "What?"

"It hit me," Kaliska frowns rubbing her bottom, "I wasn't even taking its leaves."

Alice raises a brow at the girl, and then peers at the plant in question. It's bent a little awkwardly, like an upside down U near the top, but that's not all that unusual for this type of tree, especially its saplings. Malabi's are known to be especially flexible when young.

Alice steps closer and Kaliska warns, "Careful, it could still be angry."

Alice gives her head a dubious shake and crouches down to examine the plant. It's not moving of course, but it does have an ample amount of spider silk over it, a few strands connecting it to other nearby plants. The strands are as thin as ones still clinging on Alice's fur, making her think the spinner is fairly small. Looking for it now, she can see that many of the trees have glimmering threads of silk connecting their branches, but other than that there is nothing suspicious about the sapling itself.

Alice takes the young tree between two fingers and waves it a bit to show Kaliska it's inanimate, "I don't see anything."

But the Chitali's attention has already been taken by some sort of bird roosting in a tree. It looks similar to a large pigeon though it's difficult to tell its colors in the growing darkness, maybe gray or some drab brown. It watches the girls curiously, its head bobbing. Alice, knowing their meager food stores won't last them long, readies her bow. Kaliska looks back to her with a grin, but then her expression turns to shock as she sees Alice draw back and take aim.

Just as she's about to loose her shot, the deer girl bats at her bow shouting, "No!"

The arrow zips off into the forest and the startled bird flies away.

"What the tick, Kali?!" demands Alice, looking after her lost arrow.

Kaliska frowns, asserting, "You can't kill it."

Alice glares at her, "Not if you blow my shot. What's wrong with you?"

"What's wrong with me?! You were going to shoot that bird!" Kaliska shouts as if Alice had gone mad.

"Yeah, it's called huntin', which we need to do if we wanna eat, so we can, ya know, not die?!" counters Alice.

Kaliska tears off her basket and begins shoving the leaves and grasses she's collected into Alice's chest, "Here! Eat this! And these!"

Alice tries to grab all of the deer girl's greens even while still holding her bow, "What're you doing?"

"You don't *need* to kill things!" Kaliska shouts, tears beginning to well in her eyes.

Danahlia appears from the forest followed shortly by Twinkaleni.

"What's goin' on? You two ok?" asks the Liguna.

"Alice was trying to shoot a bird!" accuses Kaliska, as if it were the most heinous crime imaginable.

Danahlia looks confused to Alice, "So, did you get it?"

"No, she threw off my shot," says Alice, nodding to the Chitali while letting the leaves fall to the ground.

Twinkaleni grumbles, "All your screaming has no doubt frightened off any more game."

"Good," sniffs Kaliska.

"How's that good?" demands Danahlia, "Our food isn't gonna last forever, we're gonna need more."

Kaliska gathers what's left in her basket and waves some greens before Danahlia, "We can eat leaves."

"But I don't like leaves," says Danahlia, pushing down the Chitali's offering, "I want meat."

Kaliska blows out a breath from her nose, then exclaims, "Fine! You all want to kill something so bad? Then kill *me*!"

"What?" the others say together as the deer girl places her basket on the ground and lies down beside it.

"Go on. You can kill me and eat me. I should keep you fed for a while. Then when you poop me out all over the mountain, I can help all kinds of things grow," she claims, baring her long, slender neck to them.

"We're not gonna eat you Kali, get up," orders Alice.

Kaliska crosses her arms, "No. Either kill me and eat me, or promise you won't kill anything else."

"Welp, I guess we gotta eat her," says Danahlia, lifting her spear.

Kaliska looks up at her with wide eyes, as Twinkaleni grumbles, "Don't be foolish. Night will be upon us soon. We should build a fire to help ward off predators, who may just decide to eat *us*."

The girls spread out to collect some fallen branches and dried leaves, though Kaliska stays put. They get a fire going beside the deer girl, who still refuses to move unless they promise not to hurt ferals. During dinner they try to convince her of the need to hunt but, being a herbivore, she refuses to acknowledge their reasoning.

"But don't you kill plants when you take their leaves?" asks Danahlia.

Kaliska, though still lying down, munches on what was dropped on the ground, "Not if you only take a few."

"You acknowledge that the consumption of one being will benefit others via droppings that aid in nurturing new life?" asks Twinakleni.

"Yes, but you can do the same while eating plants," nods the Chitali.

Nibbling on a bit of too dry fish, Alice asks, "What about ferals? They eat other ferals all the time."

"Nobodies around to teach them better," claims Kaliska.

"What about bugs, can we eat bugs?" asks Danahlia.

Kaliska grimaces, "Eww, yes, you eat all the bugs."

"What possible moral or ethical difference is there between eating ferals and insects?" asks Twinkaleni.

Kaliska is quick to reply with, "Bugs are gross."

"Have you ever eaten a bug?" wonders Alice.

The deer girl makes a disgusted face at her, "Ew, no!"

"Then how do you know they're gross?" asks Danahlia, snatching up some sort of beetle that's wandered into the fire light.

"Ugh, I can tell just by looking at them," claims Kaliska.

Danahlia looks at the beetle for a moment. "Looks fine to me," she says just before popping it into her mouth.

"Uh! You! Ughh!!" cries Kaliska, scooting away from Danahlia and into Alice.

The Liguna smiles widely at her, showing bug bits in her teeth.

"You really should be more open minded," encourages Twinkaleni.

Alice adds, "Yeah, I've eaten bugs before too."

Kaliska gives her a shocked look as Twinkaleni informs, "Some can be quite appetizing, and nutritional."

The Chitali gets some distance from the others and curls into a ball, "That's nasty, you guys are nasty," she then amends, "But as long as you're not hurting the ferals, I guess you're ok."

Reaching that compromise, the girls settle in for bed. The tarp they bought is large enough for them all to sleep on comfortably, though Alice and Danahlia lie with each other, Danahlia resting her chin on the fox girl's head. Alice sighs contentedly, finding Danahlia's chest against her back immensely comforting, and snuggles in closer. Then Kaliska scoots back into Alice from in front, shimming her way under one of Alice's arms.

"Can we help you?" asks Danahlia.

Kaliska makes herself comfortable before replying, "Nah, I'm good. Thanks though."

Alice and Danahlia share a look and Alice shrugs, stroking the Chitali's long, finely furred neck and together they fall asleep.

Chapter 9

The Wall

Early the next morning, Alice is again awoken by Kaliska, though at least this time the Chitali merely pats a hand over the sleepy fox's hip. Alice tries to ignore it, keeping her eyes shut, but this only encourages the deer girl to pat more urgently.

When she can't take it anymore, Alice finally knees her in the butt grumbling, "What?!"

"Ah, hey," cries Kaliska, rubbing her tush and frowning back at the Tokala.

They stare at each other for a moment until Alice growls through clenched teeth, "Why did you wake me up, again?"

Kaliska looks as if she just remembered something of great importance and turns to point high into some nearby trees, "Oh yeah, eyes are watching us."

"What?" Alice asks, following the girl's finger and seeing nothing unusual.

"They were just there, three of 'em, and they were glowing," the deer girl insists, spreading her fingers before her eyes for emphasis.

It's still dim this early and Alice lays her head back down, "It was probably just some feral."

"Maybe, but didn't you say something about someone telling you that eyes in this mountain try to eat you?" Kaliska replies, still looking into the trees.

Alice yawns, "Then you're on guard, and if somethin' starts to eat you, you can wake me back up."

"Right," says Kaliska as Alice drifts off.

Only a short while later, it's time to start another day. Breakfast is what's left of the shatterhead, one of their ants, and a bit of smelly fish. The girls spend the day walking along the dried river and gathering what they can from the forest, a task Kaliska is only too happy about. She truly seems to enjoy telling them about the abundance the forest has to offer and they gather plenty, mostly leaves, but also mushrooms, nuts, and a few strange fruits.

One such she calls a doogy melon, which Twinkaleni says is actually called a doogyahk according to her book. These hang from thick green vines that have climbed around tree trunks and branches. The melons are easy enough to find, looking like thin, smooth, light green cucumbers, though some can be tricky to harvest due to the height at which the melons like to grow. Alice comes up with the idea to have Twinkaleni levitate her with earth magic so she can cut them down with her sword while Danahlia and Kaliska catch the fruits as they fall. Though they have little taste, like squishier versions of the cucumbers they resemble, they do have a high water content that makes them well worth the effort. The party hasn't come across any other water sources as of yet.

On their journey to the river's mountain source they see many unusual ferals as well. The beasts here have no instinctive fear of them and would be easy to hunt if not for Kaliska screaming and shooing them away every time the opportunity arises. This frustrates the others but she refuses to stop. The Chitali does manage to find some mushrooms that she insists taste just like meat when cooked and should satisfy the girl's "need to consume the flesh of innocent creatures." When they get around to trying them, they don't taste a thing like any meat Alice has ever had and she thinks it silly that they believed a vegetarian would know what meat tastes like in the first place. But at least they're filling.

As they walk, they tend to stick close to the river. This is not only to help keep their bearing, but also because the forest seems intent on not letting them venture too far from it. Anytime they stray in their search for food and water they find themselves being struck by saplings similar to the one that got Kaliska just yesterday. The occurrences, at first, are so few that the girls take the surprising little whaps as random acts of nature, but as the day draws on, Twinkaleni especially begins to suspect they may not be random at all.

"Ah!" cries Danahlia as another Malabi slaps her forearm. Already hit several times today, the angry Liguna tries to yank up the young tree with both hands growling, "I, am getting, really, sick, of, these!"

Kaliska rushes to her, but more out of concern for the plant than Danahlia, "No! Stop! You'll just make the forest madder!"

The words are so strange they give the Liguna pause, "What?! It's a forest, it doesn't get mad!"

"Ya-huh, that's why we're being snapped at. We've angered it," insists the Chitali, taking the sapling from the lizard girl's hands and trying to stand it back up.

"How have we angered it? We just got here," asks Alice, shoulders sagging under the weight of her vegetation loaded backpack.

"I don't know, but it clearly doesn't want us going this way. We should stick close to the river," the deer girl advises. The sapling had been partially uprooted and won't stay up on its own, so Kaliska gently places it on the ground and starts digging a wider hole for it with her bare hands.

"Danny is right of course. A forest cannot become angry, but this does not apply to its inhabitance," says Twinkaleni, examining the Malabi.

"You think people live here?" wonders Danahlia, rubbing her forearm.

The tiny mouse mage looks around as she replies, "Possible, though if not people, some sort of intelligent life must. Look at this."

Twinkaleni directs them toward a commonality that all of the saplings have had thus far. A part of them have been wrapped with what might be spider's silk near their tops.

"Yeah, they've all had that," recalls Alice.

"Indeed. I thought them merely left over from some wandering spider's egg sac or some such, but look here," Twinkaleni points to another nearby Malabi with more white silk spun upon it.

"So what?" grumbles Danahlia.

Picking up the uprooted Malabi, Twinkaleni places the silk coated bit with the other's and it appears they had been torn from each other, "These two saplings where joined here, but why? There are no substantial webs around for catching prey. Why would spiders expend so much silk to bind these two saplings like this?

"To lay their eggs, like you said?" suggests Alice.

"I am reconsidering this. There is no evidence of an egg sac here, and so low and in the open is hardly a safe place for one," says Twinkaleni, and when the others can give no suitable answer she concludes, "I believe these where intentionally being used as traps, traps possibly set for us."

Danahlia makes a rude noise with her tongue, "Spiders don't make traps like that."

"None that we yet know of," says the Murin, narrowing her eyes at the taller girl, "And this is assuming it is in fact spiders who are setting them."

"What do you mean? Who else could be?" asks Alice.

"I mean there are other things that use silk," says Twinkaleni thoughtfully.

"Caterpillars use silk to make cocoons," puts in Kaliska, still digging.

Twinkaleni nods, "They do, but I was referring to the pixies back in your forest, Alice."

"Hey yeah, they liked to collect it to make stuff," agrees Danahlia.

"You think there're pixies in this forest too?" Alice asks, looking around carefully for the tiny fae's iconic lights.

"I think that whatever is crafting these traps is intelligent enough to either be trying to keep us away or lure us in," claims Twinkaleni.

The fact that they encounter more of the whip traps the further they stray from the dried river bed helps reinforce the theory, though Twinkaleni admits it may simply be due to there being fewer saplings to use nearer the river and, of course, none within. Not especially liking this talk of potentially intelligent spiders or other trap setters, the party moves on with more caution. The traps can sometimes be identified if they pay attention, but many are hidden around trees and bushes, keeping the occasional whap a surprise.

The party settles down in the river bed as evening sets in. Kaliska begins healing the small welts from the last few hours and they eat what they've gathered, plus another giant red ant for dinner. Even with the succulence of the doogy melons, the girls find it hard to quench their growing thirst as they now drink with rationing in mind, hoping the spring is not as dry as its river.

Twinkaleni spares them any training today, instead focusing intently on a doogy melon in her lap. She's removed the top of it and makes rising gestures over the melon as if mimicking smoke.

Alice watches from the fire a little ways away as Kaliska tends to her wounds.

Danahlia plops herself beside them and asks, "What's she doin' now?" But before either can answer she calls, "Hey, Twinkie! Whatcha doin'?"

The Murin mage starts, then her arms fall limply to her sides as she glares at the Liguna. "I am trying to *focus*!" she spits hotly back.

"Geez, sorry," says Danahlia, looking away to the ant and mushrooms cooking over low flames.

As Twinkaleni gets back to it, Kaliska begins rubbing her muzzle all over Alice's newly healed arm, moaning, "Mmm, all better."

"Thanks, Kali," says Alice, gently pushing the deer girl away.

The girls dig into their evening meal, though Twinkaleni continues her strange movements with what are clearly frustrating results.

After another irritated sigh from the mage, Alice waves her over to the fire, "Come and eat, Twinkaleni. We don't need you passin' out on us again."

The tiny girl shoots her an angry glare, but it softens immediately and she nods, walking over to join them by the fire. After letting Twinkaleni get some food in her belly, Alice risks asking what all her waving is about.

The mouse mage gives the doogy melon at her side a disgusted look as she replies, "I was attempting to extract the water from this doogyak's flesh."

"Why?" asks Kaliska, munching on another of the melons.

Twinkaleni lets out a groan, "Obviously, being able to extract water from vegetation would be an immensely helpful skill in situations such as we currently find ourselves."

"You get any?" asks Danahlia, giving a cooked mushroom on a stick a testing pinch.

Twinkaleni sighs, "No."

"Why not?" wonders Alice.

"Because it's difficult!" bursts Twinkaleni, startling the others. She then says a bit calmer, "You wouldn't understand. It's, it's like trying to pick up a drop of water from wet sand with your fingers, it's just too diluted and... convoluted."

Feeling a bit frustrated herself, Alice takes in a deep breath and lets it out slowly before replying, "Well, it does sound difficult. I'm sure you'll get it with practice."

"Yeah, you got mad skills, you'll get it," adds Danahlia.

Kaliska takes a close look at the melon she's eaten most of and asks, "Why not just squeeze 'em?" She gives the melon she's holding a squeeze, causing juices to drip down over her fingers.

Twinkaleni frowns, "That was my first thought, naturally, but not all plants can simply be squeezed for their water. Trees for example."

Alice raises an eyebrow, "You wanna get water from trees?"

"And why not?" the mage asks, "Consider the potential for such a spell. As long as there are suitable plants about, we may not have to worry about water again. With sufficient mastery, we would only need to carry a single cup to drink from, perhaps not even that. No longer would we be ladened with heavy waterskins everywhere we go. No longer would we need to search for streams or hope for rain when I could simply pull it from local flora."

"I never heard o' anything like that. Is it even possible?" asks Danahlia.

"I believe it is," assures Twinkaleni, she then looks distastefully at the melon she had been experimenting on before grabbing it up and biting into it. She then says with a full mouth, "Alish has dah right of it, it's merely a madah of fractice."

And practice she does, long into the night. Even as the others huddle together to sleep, the determined Murin sits by the fire, making her smoke-like gestures with her fingers and arms over another melon. Sleepy, Alice watches her work. She'd asked the Murin to give it up for the night repeatedly, but each time Twinkaleni had refused with ever increasing hostility. This worries the young fox, though Danahlia insists she obsesses every time she wants to learn some new magic, adding that it's probably what's made her so powerful even at such a young age.

As she yawns and her eyelids get heavier, Alice notices the soft, bluish white light of stars peeking through the darkness. She looks at these for a moment before realizing that the forest's thick canopy should be blocking them from view. Curiously, she observes the lights, wondering if they may be some reflection off leaves or even dew. Then one of them moves away from the others.

"What's that?" she says, pointing to them.

This snaps Twinkaleni from her focus and she looks to where the Tokala indicates before shouting, "Estra Mishraities!"

The mage looks as if she throws glittering powder into the air that hangs midflight in a cloud of light. Hers is pure white and should be distinct from the blue but searching the branches, they see nothing.

"Did you see them? The little blue lights?" asks Alice.

Danahlia mumbles, "What?"

Twinkaleni nods, "Indeed. It appears we are not alone."

"The eyes, the eyes are back. They're gonna eat us," cries Kaliska, rising to shake the Tokala with both hands.

"I highly doubt that. Judging by their movements and positions among the trees, they're probably just some small nocturnal ferals scrounging about under cover of darkness," assures Twinkaleni, quickly resuming her attempts to free water from a melon.

Alice manages to take hold of both of the deer girl's wrists, trying to still her as Kaliska looks worriedly around the trees and cries, "What if it's not and they want to eat us?"

"Let 'em come. I'll eat them first," claims Danahlia, still lying on her back.

"Why don't you stand guard then," Alice tells the Chitali, motioning to Twinkaleni.

"Yeah, yeah, ok," says Kaliska, getting up to walk to Twinkaleni, while still looking about the dark forest, the Murin's light spell fading.

Alice settles back down on her side, watching Kaliska sit by Twinkaleni. Danahlia places herself at her back and drapes an arm and a leg over her with a pleased sigh. Alice smiles and snuggles back into the larger girl to get her head into the cozy little nook against the Liguna's neck and under her jaw. From this safe, comfortable place, she watches Kaliksa steadily scoot, inch by inch, closer to Twinkaleni until the weariness of the day claims her and she falls asleep.

Waking up the next morning, Danahlia and Alice find Kaliska somehow cuddled up with Twinkaleni. The mage's head rests on Kaliska's belly, while the deer girl loosely holds the tiny Murin's expansive ears, one in either hand. Alice and Danahlia share a grin and try to wake the pair up for breakfast.

Kaliska starts, her eyes flashing open as her hands dart all over her body, "They didn't eat me did they?"

"Doesn't look like it," says Alice, mock checking the girl over as well.

Twinkaleni grumbles and rolls over to settle back into sleep.

"See, this is what happens when you play with magic all night instead of gettin' your rest like a good little mage," chides Danahlia.

Twinkaleni sleeps through breakfast and the girls decide it's best to keep moving while they still have some water to drink. Danahlia bundles the Murin in the tarp and holds her to her back like a baby.

As they begin their journey anew, Kaliska yawns and looks enviously at Twinkaleni, then pleadingly to Alice who immediately states, "I am not going to carry you."

While they follow the river bed, Danahlia takes her usual lead position, even carrying her precious cargo, while Alice sticks close to her side. Kaliska trails, bounding between bushes and trees, picking various leaves while telling the others how they can be eaten, brewed into tea, or used to make remedies.

Alice ends up watching Twinkaleni, completely relaxed in sleep on Danahlia's back. The Murin's mouth is partially opened with a bit of spittle staining the tarp below it.

Danahlia suddenly stops and points, "Check that out."

Following the gesture, Alice spots a doogy melon floating in midair. Looking at a slightly different angle lets the sunlight reveal that it's actually hanging from a high tree branch by nearly invisible strands of silk. As the two are observing this odd occurrence, Kaliska comes up to Alice and begins telling her of some new leaves she's collected that are supposed to whiten teeth and freshen breath. Alice blindly reaches for the prattling deer girl, still examining the strange scene, and manages to clamp a hand over her muzzle to muffle her talking.

"Another trap?" Alice whispers to Danahlia.

"Looks like. Seriously, how dumb do they think we are?" Danahlia whispers back.

Kaliska pulls free her mouth and grumbles, "Hey," and then seeing the fruit she cheers, "Hey! Floating food."

Alice shushes her, warning, "It could be another trap."

"Or, ooor, it could be a reward for staying near the river like the forest wanted," says Kaliska.

"That's… yeah, that's right, it could be. Why don't you go collect our reward," says Danahlia, putting a hand on the Chitali's shoulder and giving her an encouraging push.

"Ok!" cheers Kaliska, bounding toward the hanging melon.

"Wait, Kal-" Alice starts after her but Danahlia holds a hand before her chest. Alice looks to the Liguna who continues to observe cautiously.

Kaliska pulls the fruit from the strands of web easily enough and shakes it for the others to see before returning to them. Removing the silk, she immediately bites into it only to have Alice slap it from her hands.

"Ugh! What the tick!" cries Kaliska, kneeling to pick it up.

"It might be poisoned or something, Kali! Geez, don't you think it's strange, at all, that there's a piece of fruit just hanging here for us to find?" exclaims Alice.

"Uh, no. All the fruit we've found so far have been hanging. It'd be stranger if it wasn't," Kaliska argues, brushing some dirt off her doogyak.

"She has a point," grins Danahlia, "How's it taste, Kali?"

"It's ok I guess," the deer girl replies, looking down at her soiled fruit.

"It doesn't taste funny or anything?" asks Alice.

Kaliska takes another bite and then frowns, "It tastes sad, probably because you made me drop it."

No one has a response to this and they continue on their way.

The girls find several more hanging fruit, one after another all along the river. Kaliska gleefully collects them to no ill effect which makes Alice and Danahlia all the more suspicious. The two suspect who ever left the fruit might be trying to lead them somewhere, perhaps hoping the free food will lower their guard. Twinkaleni wakes up groggily before noon and reports she had made little progress with her water extraction spell despite being at it all night. As they explain to her the new situation, Alice notices the ground having a slight cool wetness to it. Danahlia agrees and even she encourages caution when Kaliska continues to find more hanging melons along their path.

Still, nothing negative happens, though the ground gets wetter and wetter as they venture on. Encouraged that they could finally be closing in on the source of the river, the girls try to contain their excitement as they remain vigilant. Soon the silt at their feet is mud and they walk along the shore to avoid it. Green grasses are growing thickly here and it's a vast improvement to the rocks of the river bottom. As they press on, they find small puddles, much too dirty to drink from, but morale boosting none the less. Unconsciously, they begin to increase their pace, eager for their water hunt to be over.

Excitement building, they begin to race each other as the puddles, most near the center of the river bed, steadily form into pools of ever increasing size. Twinkaleni, quickly outpaced by the others, unleashes her wind running spell and the girls fly forth, caution forgotten in the simple thrill of finally finding drinking water. Lungs heaving but laughing, Alice runs past her friends only to stop before a strange barrier. A dense wall of what looks like green surface roots, dotted with fist sized pods, blocks the entire river and extends far onto the shore on either side. More of the root-like tendrils reach out from the base of the wall for several yards giving it a sloping face. The ground is the most saturated where the roots are, though no water readily leaks free anywhere.

"What, is this?" huffs Danahlia when she catches up.

"I guess, its why, the rivers, gone dry," gasps Alice, stooping over.

Kaliska comes bounding up next, calling encouragingly to Twinkaleni to make her wind blow harder. The mage brings up the rear, charging at a full tilt, arms waving in the air and clearly off balance. She's unable to stop her momentum, causing her to run right into Danahlia's leg. The tiny Murin bounces off to land in the grass with a startled squeak. The wind suddenly dies off and Alice helps the mouse girl to her feet.

"Oh, what is that?" wonders Kaliska, staring in awe at the giant, green wall.

Alice looks to their plant expert, "You don't know what it is?"

"Nope nope, this ones new to me," says Kaliska, taking a few steps toward it.

"What about you, Mini-Mage?" Danahlia asks Twinkaleni.

The smallest of the group narrows her eyes at the Liguna while brushing herself off and then examines the plant barrier, "I am unfamiliar with this particular plant as well."

The girls approach it, looking curiously at the leafless root plant and its pods. The root parts look like any other root, save for being green. The pods however look like some sort of fruit. They have red and orange skin and taper somewhat like a pear, though the smaller end is exposed to the air while the bulbous end is attached to the plant by a thick, fleshy stem. As Danahlia steps over some of the roots to reach for the closest pod, all those around it turn toward her and squirt a thread thin stream of liquid from their tapered ends with startling force and accuracy. The Liguna cries out in surprise, back peddling, her hands coming up to her face.

"Danny!" Alice gasps, reaching for her, "What happened? Are you ok?"

"Ah! My eyes!" Danahlia cries out, rubbing at them. Twinkaleni pulls a spare shirt from her backpack and offers it, only to have the Liguna's flailing tail knock it out of her hand.

"Eyes," says Kaliska, her own widening, "Althea said to watch our eyes! Oh no! Was it acid? Are you blind?! Are your eyes melting?!" the deer girl shouts as she attempts to hold lizard girl steady with Alice and lead her away from the offending plants.

"No, it just *really* stings," exclaims Danahlia, taking the recovered shirt from Twinkaleni.

After a few moments, Alice asks to see and Danahlia pulls away the cloth to reveal her eyes are an angry red with purple around the edges, the delicate flesh around them puffy and swollen.

Alice looks to the Chitali,"Kali, can you heal her?"

"Uhhhhh, maybe," she replies uncertainly, inspecting Danahlia's face.

"Does it hurt anywhere else?" Alice asks.

"Nah, just where it got in my eyes. Ugh, it stings," she exclaims, pushing Kaliska away when the deer girl licks her cheek.

"Lemons," Kaliska says distastefully, sticking her tongue out with a bitter face as Danahlia rapidly blinks.

Alice sniffs at the Liguna, particularly where some of the liquid has beaded on her skin, finding it does smell of lemons.

"Some sort of defense mechanism," says Twinkaleni, eyeing the pods, "Clever, for a plant. I imagine this must be what's blocking the flow of the river.

"Let's kill it then. Twinkie, torch it," orders Danahlia, still blinking.

Twinkaleni frowns but summons a stream of fire that she rakes over the plant barrier. Other than browning the root like structure, the spell has little effect. The Murin mage announces that, as she suspected, the roots are far too saturated for fire to do much damage. Then she has a thought and fires another thin beam of flame at one of the pods. After several seconds under the intense heat, the pod bursts, puffing free a cloud of steam.

"Good job," cheers Alice, and the Murin grins in satisfaction.

"Yeah, that's one way to do it. Think you have enough fire in you to pop all of 'em?" asks Danahlia.

"Given time," replies Twinkaleni, looking at the possibly hundreds of pods.

"How about just these," Alice says, panning a finger from the base to the top of the wall, "I wanna climb it, see how thick it is."

"Shouldn't be difficult," says Twinkaleni confidently, before calling, "Feasta!"

The Murin mage fires streams of flame with both hands at two separate pods near the base of the wall. When they pop, she moves on to two more further along Alice's intended path. Meanwhile, Alice accepts Danahlia's offered cloak. She drops her pack, while Kaliska takes another look at the Liguna's eyes. Alice takes only her sword and the cloak before she begins scaling the root wall.

Twinkaleni does a fair job of clearing a narrow path through the squirting pods, but still many, even those several feet away, react to Alice's presence by firing their mildly acidic juices at her. The fox girl keeps low as she climbs, the roots thick enough to make the assent easy. She feels the force of the pods' attacks like being poked with twigs and the cloak begins to moisten with the assault. The lemony scent gets stronger and stronger as more pods unleash their fury upon her, though to no great hindrance. She has to stop and wait several times for Twinkaleni to clear the path, but she reaches the top in only a few minutes.

Hands and feet dripping with sticky pod juice, Alice looks over the wall, only to duck down again as pods turn toward her and fire at her face. She waits out their attack, squirts coming in bursts that slowly lessen in length and strength until the pods are spent. Only then does she risks another glance, to see a most bizarre sight. It's a battle, she thinks.

Spiders, perhaps only just larger than Alice's open hand, are dropping down on their threads over more of the root plant's pods. Many have tiny bluish figures astride them. Some of the spiders who have managed to get close enough to the pods have begun wrapping them in cocoons of silk and force them to aim away from their kin, while their riders seem to be trying to damage the pods' stems. Many of the figures and spiders alike are being hit with the needle thin jets of pod juice. For such small creatures, the force is enough to send them flying off in different directions. As if it wasn't strange enough, none of the small creatures present create any noise, making the conflict an eerily silent affair.

Alice watches as a spider and its rider, descending on a thread, are hit. The spider rocks wildly from the blast, launching the tiny figure right before her. Instinctively, she extends a hand and catches the figure before it can fall over the side of the root wall. Its weight is so slight, she isn't sure she caught it until she brings her hand around to look. The figure is minuscule, smaller even than most pixies she'd met, at only two knuckles high. It looks somewhat like a person though its body is clear as if made from water. Looking closer, she can see its heart beating right through its tiny chest as it stirs. The figure raises its water droplet shaped head and Alice sees what she thought was a drop of pod juice is actually attached to the figure's head via a hair thin antenna of some sort.

The figure looks around noticing Alice's fingers and then darts its gaze up. Alice smiles but the figure looks terrified and scoots back a few centimeters while the droplet on the end of its antenna begins to blink rapidly with a blue light. The light reminds her of something but before the thought can form, one of the spiders lands on her hand. Not being particularly fond of spiders in general, Alice shrieks, tossing both away and losing her grip on the wall. She flails but can't get a hold and begins to fall.

Chapter 10

In the Mud

Alice free falls to the voices of her frightened friends calling to her, just before Twinkaleni shouts, "Asendiote!"

The familiar grip of the mage's gravity spell forms about the Tokala to pull her from the wall and steadily bring her down.

"Alice! Are you ok? Those pods get you?" Danahlia asks as Alice gets her feet back on the ground.

"No. Thanks, Twinkaleni. There were people up there, tiny ones, and spiders, and I think they were fightin' the pods," explains Alice, gesturing with her hands.

Kaliska claps excitedly, "Tiny people? Like pixies?"

Alice shakes her head, "I don't know, they looked like people, but clear like water. I only saw one up close for a second, but it didn't have wings. A spider jumped on me and I fell."

"What did you say these people were doing again?" wonders Twinkaleni.

"I think they were tryin' to fight this plant thing by attackin' the pods, but they were gettin' shot down all over," Alice tells her friends, gesturing some more.

"With spiders?" the Murin asks, one brow raised.

Alice nods, "Yeah, the tiny people were ridin' 'em."

"You hit your head on the way down didn't you?" asks Danahlia.

"No, it's true," Alice insist, tossing the damp cloak to her, "Go look."

Danahlia catches it, purses her lips, and then puts it on before turning to scale the wall. Excited, Kaliska turns to follow, wrapping the shirt over her head. While the two make their way up, Alice explains what she saw in greater detail to Twinkaleni, who continues popping the abundant pods with her fire magic. After as detailed a description as she can give, Alice asks the Murin what she thinks the little people might be.

Experimenting between using wide cones of flame to roast several pods and focused beams to pop one at a time, Twinkaleni replies, "I can't say for sure without a detailed analysis, but they may very well be some kind of forest sprite."

"Sprite? Is that a fae, like the pixies?" asks Alice as she draws her sword to carefully slice a few of the pods closest to the ground.

But before the mouse mage can answer, Kaliska calls down excitedly, "Hey, I got one! It's a thing, with a thingy!"

They look up to see her half turned around with something in one hand while the other makes gestures that look like she's trying to pluck spider web from her ears.

"Float me, float me!" she calls just before leaping from the top of the wall.

"Wha-? Wait, Asendiote!" cries Twinkaleni, catching the deer girl in midair with her magic.

Danahlia climbs down as Kaliska floats to the ground and they gather to look into her hand. Then they crouch so Twinkaleni can see too. Kaliska has managed to catch another of the tiny people.

"Is it dead?" wonder Danahlia, looking at the still figure.

Kaliska looks closer, "I don't know, it just landed on me."

"Probably shot down by one o' those pods," says Alice.

"Yeah, these guys and their spiders are gettin' thrashed up there," agrees Danahlia.

"Most fascinating," says Twinkaleni, "Its epidermis is entirely transparent."

"And its skin's clear," adds Kaliska, "What do you think that's for?" she asks, pointing to the bobble at the end of its single antenna.

"It lights up blue," says Alice, just as the minuscule figure stirs.

Like the first Alice had seen, this one too wakes in fright. Realizing it's surrounded, the little bobble begins to blink rapidly. And though its heart races in its tiny chest, the figure makes no sound.

"Bioluminescence," says Twinkaleni in awe, "Perhaps it is how they communicate, similar to firefl-ah!"

Before she can finish the thought, a spider drops amid the girl's closely pressed faces. They all cry out and fall back, Kaliska inadvertently launching the tiny figure into the air. The spider manages to catch it and immediately begins climbing back up its thread to the safety of a tree branch above.

Twinkaleni shudders, "Why spiders?"

Watching the spider disappear among the leaves from on her back, Alice asks, "So did it look like a sprite?"

"A what?" wonder Danahlia.

Twinkaleni says it might have been and then goes on to say that sprites are another type of lesser fae, similar to pixies but often wingless. "They, with their, ugh, spiders, may very well have been the ones setting those traps and even leaving those doogyaks for us to find."

"Yeah," agrees Alice, "It's like they wanted to lure us here, but why?"

"They need help," affirms Kaliska, "They want us to get rid of this rooty sour squirter wall."

"Makes sense," says Danahlia, "It's thick, but I'm pretty sure it's what's blockin' the river. We break up this thing and Fiske 'll have its water back."

"We may also gain the opportunity to learn about the local inhabitance," adds Twinkaleni.

"This thing blocks rivers and squirts lemon juice. If Althea were here, she'd say it's evil. We need to destroy it!" cries Kaliska, raising a fist in the air.

For once agreeing with the Chitali, the others raise a fist too, still lying on their backs.

After a minute, they get back to their feet and start to come up with a plan for their daunting task. The first thing they need to do is get rid of the pods. Alice uses her sword to fashion long spears from branches, and the girls use their length to keep out of range of the pods as they pierce them. All it takes is a sharp poke to cause the pods to leak. Without being able to build any pressure, the pods can't fire and quickly shrivel.

Once an area is cleared, Danahlia and Alice begin pulling at the root like mass of the plant while Kaliska and Twinkaleni continue expanding their safe zone. Most of the tendrils are less than wrist thick, fairly hollow, and brittle, giving way with a few good yanks. When broken, watery, lemon scented sap leaks readily from them, making the girl's hands unpleasantly sticky.

An exhausting hour later and nearly draining their water supply, Twinkaleni suggests they clear a path over the wall so they can restock. With the four of them working together, it doesn't take long to manage. The tiny people and spiders have ceased their attack and have disappeared into the trees, leaving many pods tangled in webbing. Kaliska decides to collect these and no one questions it. The plant wall is several yards thick and beyond it the river has flooded, leaving the water murky and full of various floating bits that are determined not to settle.

"We'll want to filter this somehow before drinking it," advises Twinkaleni.

They consider this for a moment before Alice has an idea, "Hey Kali, lemme see your basket."

The Chitali carefully removes it and hands it over just for Alice to dump its contents on the ground.

"Hey," the deer girl cries, reaching for it.

"We just need it for a minute," says Alice apologetically, pulling it away from her.

She then presses the basket into the water. The weave of it is tight but not water proof and slowly begins to fill with clean water.

"Not bad, Foxy," says Danahlia approvingly, removing the cap of a waterskin.

As the girls top off their supply, drink, and refill Kaliska's basket, the Chitali takes one of her web wrapped pods and jams a finger through the hole left by the stem. She then pours some of the juice into a water skin, gives it a shake and then drinks it. She sticks out her tongue with a sour face and then digs around in her basket for what looks like some sort of fern. After rolling some of its leaves around in her hand, she adds this to her concoction and takes another drink.

This time she smiles and says, "Slightly less terrible."

"Uh, you know the pod's juice might be poisonous or somethin', right?" asks Alice.

Kaliska rolls her eyes, "Ugh, what is it with you and everything being poisonous? Althea didn't say anything about poison, so we don't have to worry about it."

"Oh, well, if *Althea* neglected to mention weird poisonous plants, I'm sure it's wags to put everythin' and anythin' out here in our mouths," says Danahlia sarcastically.

Kaliska nods, "Now you're getting it," and starts back to the base of the wall.

"Ya know, I'm glad she came," comments Danahlia.

Twinkaleni adds, "Indeed. She will be useful for testing the toxicity of local flora."

Danahlia laughs, "Was that a joke?"

Twinkaleni grins and starts after the Chitali, as do the others.

The four pull and cut their way through the wall until late in the evening. They work on making a fairly thin passage right in the middle of the wall, Twinkaleni suggesting that once they break through, the pent up water may help carry some of the rest with it. Near the base of the wall are older, thicker tendrils that the girls take turns chopping at with Alice's sword while the others pull away the younger thinner ones. It's when Danahlia is pulling at some of these higher up that a jet of water bursts through. Alice, chopping below, has to flee from getting soaked and the girls cheer for the progress they've made. After, tired and with plenty more to go, they decide to call it a day.

With no ready supply of water till now, the party had managed to get rather dirty and decide to use the water jet as a shower. Danahlia insists on going first, stripping down immediately, while the others collect materials for a fire. As Alice is stacking wood into a pile, Danahlia cries out in surprise and then whoops in joy. Alice looks to see the Liguna crouch to pick up a decent sized river trout flopping about at her feet.

"Where'd that come from?" the fox girl asks.

"It just shot outta here," Danahlia says, indicating the water jet, "Looks like we're havin' fish tonight!"

Kaliska drops her armful of sticks and runs toward the lizard girl crying, "Oh, no, we need to get it back into the water."

As the Chitali reaches for the fish, Danahlia turns away, keeping it from her grasping hands, "Whoa, no way! I'm eatin' it!"

"No, you can't!" Kaliska shouts, trying to climb over a nude Danahlia.

The Liguna gets a hand and tail on her to keep her away, "Kali, look, this is not an ordinary fish."

"Give it! It's gonna die!" Kaliska screams, still reaching for the fish.

"Kali, listen to me! This is a fate fish. It was chosen by the god of this river as a reward for us."

"No!" the deer girl persists.

Danahlia shoves her away and she falls back onto her bottom, getting soaked by the water jet, "Kali! This fish was given to us as thanks for our work to clear the river god's home of this evil plant thing. Do you really want to refuse a gift from a god?"

Kaliska looks around uncertainly, "No, but, it'll die."

Danahlia nods, "Yes it will, but its spirit will be happy because it did what the river god wanted."

The deer girl sniffs, "But-"

Danahlia puts up a finger, "And, it'll get a special place in the river god's heart for this, isn't that a good thing?"

Kaliska frowns, on the verge of tears, "How do you know?"

"Because the river god told me, just now while I was showering," claims the Liguna.

Kaliska looks around more urgently, "Where? Where's the river god?"

"Duh, in the river. He spoke to me through the water," says Danahlia.

"Nuh-uh," Kaliska replies, getting to her hooves.

"Yeah, come over here, he might say somethin' else," says Danahlia, positioning the deer girl before the jet where she was just standing while grinning at Alice over her shoulder.

Alice and Twinkaleni share a humored look just before the mage lights the fire.

Now getting thoroughly soaked, Kaliska shouts over the patter of water, "I don't hear anything."

Making her way to the fire, Danahlia calls back, "He might have gone upriver. Gods get busy, ya know?" Then she adds, "Oh, and the river god also said, once we take down this wall, its wags if we take all the fish we want, as a thank you."

It's some time before Kaliska gives up on listening for the river god and actually starts to bathe, revealing that she was indeed wearing nothing beneath her robe and that she has a cute, leaf shaped tail that's golden on top and white on its underside. As everyone takes their turn, they're blessed with another trout from Danahlia's river god. The killing, cooking, and eventual eating of the fish clearly upsets the Chitali and despite being soaked, she keeps her distance from the "flesh eaters" and their fire. They offer her dry clothes, her only piece now wet, but she refuses with a mix of grief and anger, and then starts to sneeze.

"Come on Kali, at least sit by the fire, you're gonna catch a cold," pleads Alice.

Kaliska sniffs, "No, I will not share a ah (sneeze) fire with meat eaters."

She sneezes funny, like a surprised goose, and it's hard not to smile as Alice insists she join them. After several more refusals, Alice calls on Twinkaleni, who uses her earth magic to levitate the deer girl, bringing her closer to the fire. Kaliska kicks and screams but Alice and Danahlia manage to get her out of her still damp robe and wrap her in the tarp. She settles down then and Twinkaleni places her on the ground, though she's shaking terribly. Alice holds her until she stops before returning to dinner.

Eating the trout is a long missed experience to be savored. Still warm from the fire, the oily skin breaks readily before Alice's sharp, canine teeth and she pauses to inhale, letting the heat fill her lungs. Then she bites down into flaky, pink flesh that she pulls clean from the bones, chewing slowly so her tongue can dance with the hot juices she squeezes from the meat. Only then does she swallow, feeling the warmth nestling into her stomach, satisfying the primal urge to consume and draw strength from the flesh of others. When she opens her eyes, the girls are eyeing her strangely.

Danahlia smirks, "Really enjoyin' that fish, huh?"

Alice makes a moan of agreement, unable to stop long enough for words.

"How can you eat that?" asks Kaliska, appalled, "That used to be a living, breathing, animal, with thoughts and feelings, and maybe babies."

Alice makes more pleased noises and Danahlia translates, "It's really good."

Once the girls have had their fill, it's become dark. Danahlia and Alice snuggle together as they often do now. Kaliska offers a prayer to the water still spraying from the leak in the wall, thanking the river god for the fish her friends had eaten and hoping their spirits are happy. She speaks into her hands, letting the water wash away her words when she's done. As she makes her way back to the others, the water suddenly stops flowing.

The girls look to each other curiously and Twinkaleni, practicing her water siphoning spell on another doogy melon, offers, "Something has finally clogged the leak, no doubt."

"No doubt," repeats Danahlia over Alice's head.

Kaliska whispers something to Twinkaleni, who nods. The deer girl then sits directly behind the mage, spreading her legs around the much smaller girl, to begin gently rubbing the Murin's large ears. Twinkaleni, who generally disdains physical contact, letting the Chitali touch her at all, let alone approvingly, comes as a surprise to the other two, who can't help but stare.

Twinkaleni notices, "What?" she then raises her chin to them, "It aids in my focus."

"Perks of havin' her around I guess," says Danahlia, more to Alice than anyone.

"I guess," Alice grins, "Hey, have you noticed no one's had nightmares since we found Kali?"

Danahlia lets out a thoughtful, "Hmm," and hugs Alice closer before they fall asleep.

It's still night when Alice wakes with a start to something thudding against her leg. She immediately regrets lifting her head for a look around. Pain from sore muscles reverberates in her neck down into her chest and arms and she falls back with a groan. She feels around and finds a doogy melon beside her thigh. Danahlia shifts behind her but doesn't wake. Alice takes in a breath, trying not to move for the Liguna's sake and looks up at the many stars in the sky. As she watches them, she notices some of them disappearing. She shifts her head slightly, thinking the leaves of the trees or perhaps some clouds are blocking her view, but then she notices others are moving. Still groggy but awake enough to know this isn't right, Alice looks more carefully at a gathering of stars nearest each other. And in the collective bluish white light she can see the silhouettes of what must be spiders.

Her eyes widen at the possibility that each of the several dozen lights among the trees might be accompanied by one of the hand sized arachnids. A shiver ripples over her but seeing as they have done nothing yet, she considers they may be friendly. The others still asleep, Alice decides to give diplomacy a try and offers a slight wave to the lights. As she does, some of the lights dim while others go out completely, so she stops. After a few seconds, the lights slowly return to full strength. Judging by their size, none seem to be getting any closer which offers the Tokala some relief. Next she tries talking to them.

"Hello?"

Some of the lights dim again.

"Can you speak?"

A few of the lights blink, then others at various intervals.

"Is blinking how you talk?" Alice asks.

More blinking, then Danahlia grumbles, "Alice? What the tick? Who are you talkin' to?"

Alice points, "Danny, look, the light sprites are back."

Danahlia starts to rise, "The what? Ah! Oh my neck."

Alice looks over at her, muscles aching with the effort, "Are you ok?"

Danahlia lets out a pained groan as she settles back down, "Ah, yeah, just, oh, those guys? Ugh, what do they want?

"I don't know. They're just watchin' us."

"Ugh, well tell 'em to go away."

"I don't think they can talk."

Danahlia mumbles something unintelligible before going still and silent. Alice watches the lights for a time, but the harder she tries to stay awake, the heavier her eyelids get, and she soon falls back to sleep.

The next morning, everyone is achy and sore from the day before. The lights are gone but the girls find several doogy melons hanging from spider silk around their camp.

Danahlia pulls one free, "What'd you think this is about?"

"The light sprites must have left 'em last night," says Alice, pulling the webbing off another.

"Light sprites? An apt name," says Twinkaleni, looking at the melons but not tall enough to reach them.

"Light sprites, light sprites, brightening up the night. Light sprites, light sprites, oh they're such a sight," sings Kaliska, skipping around camp as she plucks the other melons off their web lines, "They must want to be friends. I hope they come by again."

"That, or they desire to keep us here long enough to complete our work," suggests Twinkaleni.

Once Kaliska has the last of the fruit, she immediately flops on the ground and groans, "I'm tired and sore all over."

"Same here," says Danahlia, biting into a melon.

"Yeah," agrees Alice, "Is there anything you can do for us?"

Kaliska purses her lips, "Mmmm, maybe," she then spots the girl's small iron pot,"Ooo, let's make painaway tea."

"What's that?" Alice asks.

"It's tea, I forgot the real name, but I know how to make it. It's good for achiness."

The girls dump the contents of a few of their water skins into the pot and revive their fire from embers. Kaliska pulls an assortment of leaves from her collection and places them into the pot, which is then set over the fire. They have breakfast while they wait for the tea to brew.

After, Danahlia climbs the wall to fetch more water and comments from atop it, "Ticks, clearing this thing is gonna take forever."

Twinkaleni calls up to her, "I doubt we will have to do it all ourselves. I believe if we can remove the larger roots, the structure will lose stability and collapse under the pressure of the river."

Meanwhile, Kaliska hums to herself while waiting for the tea as Alice stretches out her legs to test their soreness. Kaliska takes notice and offers to help. Not sure what to expect, Alice agrees. The Chitali begins by clapping and vigorously rubbing her hands together. Tongue sticking out of one side of her mouth, she begins to roughly massage one of Alice's sore calves. It hurts at first but Alice refuses to complain and, after a few seconds, is rewarded with tingling warmth emanating from Kaliska's palms. As she rubs, Alice can feel the ache in her muscles slowly fad away to be replaced with a soothing, relaxing feeling. Kaliska steadily works up her leg and the wonderful sensation climbs with her.

Unable to help herself, Alice lets out a little moan of pleasure and gets a quick grin from the deer girl. She gets about to mid-thigh before switching legs and the warm feeling fades without the Chitali's massaging, but isn't replaced by the ache of sore muscles. Alice flexes her leg and wiggles her toes, the limb feeling wonderfully rejuvenated.

Alice moans again as the warmth spreads through her other calf, "Ohhh, Kali, you're incredible. With you healin' us up, we can get the river cleared in no time."

Kaliska doesn't respond, instead focused completely on her work. Alice lays back and enjoys the sensation. The warmth is centered on her legs but spreads throughout, relaxing her entire body like a comforting blanket. Alice can't help but smile.

Danahlia leaps down from the wall with a load of full water skins. "Hey, what's all this?" she asks, waggling a finger at them.

"Kali's healin' the ache in my legs. It's amazing," Alice grins up at her.

Danahlia raises a brow, "Oh yeah? Do me next would ya? I'm all kinds o' sore."

"Yeah, I can pro-," Kaliska collapses over Alice.

"Kali? Kali?" calls the fox girl, looking down at her.

Danahlia crouches and gives the deer girl a shake, "Hey, you ok?"

Kaliska doesn't respond.

"Mana fatigue," says Twinkaleni from where she sits with her legs crossed, a doogyak in her lap as she tries to siphon water from it. "She should really be more careful."

"Pff, didn't I have to carry you around all day just yesterday because you pooped yourself out?" retorts Danahlia, flipping Kaliska onto her back.

Twinkaleni narrows her eyes at the Liguna then returns to her work as Alice looks over the passed out Chitali and tries to position her more comfortably.

"Think she's alright?" Alice wonders.

Danahlia grumbles, "I'm sure she's fine. No heal-y massage for me."

Once the tea is done, or they think it's done because the water has turned brown, the girls take it from the fire and let it cool before having some. It's terribly bitter but they all have a few sips, being sure to save some for when Kaliska wakes up. Not terribly eager to get back to their arduous task, the party discusses what to do. Eventually, they agree for Alice and Danahlia to scout the area while Twinkaleni looks after the Chitali. Taking their weapons, the pair head into the mountain forest.

They try to skirt around the flooded area beyond the wall. The root tendrils reach far around, but look to prefer the edge of the water. As they're toes squish in the grass and damp earth, Danahlia gives Alice's tail a tug.

"Ah, hey!" the Tokala cries back as Danahlia grins.

Alice reaches for the Liguna's lengthy appendage to return it, but Danahlia deftly dodges away and begins running along the shore laughing. Alice gives chase, ignoring the bits of mud flying back at her from Danahlia's pattering feet while reaching for her waving tail. Her fingers just graze the very tip when Danahlia suddenly goes rigid. Alice can't stop her momentum and crashes into her back, taking them both to the ground.

Their "Oofs," as they splat into the shore line are answered by a deep and angry hiss. Alice looks up to see a massive set of jaws, filled with long, pointed teeth. They belong to the great lizard they nearly fell over. The Liguna tries to back pedal with her hands and feet but with Alice atop her, all she manages is to kick up mud. Perhaps even more startled than they were, the creature turns away, retreating into the water on four squat legs. Alice rolls off the larger girl and into the wet grass.

"That was, close," she huffs, feeling her heart racing.

"Yeah," Danahlia answers, flipping over to reveal her entire front covered in mud, "Swimmin' would probably be a bad idea." Then after a moment she asks, "Wanna try to hunt one?"

Alice looks over to her in surprise, "What? You wanna eat that thing? Do you even know what it is?"

"I know it's made o' meat, and meat we can eat," Danahlia grins back.

"You don't have any problems eating another lizard?" Alice asks, curious.

Danahlia rolls to her side, propped up on an elbow, "What do you mean 'another lizard'?"

Alice cocks an eyebrow, "Well, because, you know, you're a-"

"Whoa! I am *not* a lizard, I am a *Liguna*, world o' difference," insists Danahlia.

Alice mimics her posture, "Like what?"

Danahlia pulls back her head, insulted, "Uh, well, can a lizard do this?"

She runs her clawed hands through the mud, gathering up a handful to splatter all over Alice's relatively clean blouse. Alice gasps and then immediately gathers a fist full herself and adds it to Danahlia's already covered chest. It instantly becomes a contest of who can cover the other in the most mud and they sit up to get both their hands involved.

Once they each have a thick coat, Danahlia plops a handful right on Alice's head, making her cry, "Ok! Truce! You're not a lizard!"

Alice tries to wipe away the mud but Danahlia holds it in place, rubbing it into the fur about her ears, demanding, "What am I?"

Alice has to keep her eyes tightly shut as it drips down around her muzzle and shouts, "A Liguna!"

"Darn right, Fur Face," says Danahlia, sweeping the mud from Alice's head.

Alice shakes vigorously from where she sits, flinging mud all about her. She then wipes the gritty goop from her eyes with a bit of her inner blouse and opens them to see Danahlia grinning at her from only a few inches away, dripping with mud. Alice smiles, looking into the Liguna's glittering green eyes as Danahlia's grin widens, a hand coming up to wipe some mud from Alice's cheek. Alice, in turn, places her hand at the end of Danahlia's lower jaw and slowly moves back to her throat, clearing the mud while feeling the lizard girl's smooth skin.

It's then that Danahlia glides her hand from Alice's cheek to the back of her neck and gives the slightest pull as if tentatively asking for her to come closer. Alice accepts the invitation and leans in, not entirely sure what to expect. Danahlia does the same, closing the distance between them to only an inch. Alice's eyes are wide with uncertainty, and Danahlia's breaths are warm and quick on her chin. Then Danahlia turns her head slightly to the side and they kiss.

It's a rather strange sensation, lasting only a second. Alice had never kissed anyone on the lips before. It's a gritty thing, cool and tasting of mud, but somehow manages to be wonderfully warm all the same. A wave of wobbly heat glides through her body, leaving goose flesh and making her feel weak all over.

As Danahlia pulls away, she gives Alice's nose the tiniest lick and grins widely, "Well, I guess that means you like me."

Alice looks away, feeling embarrassed for some reason, but unable to keep from smiling, "Maybe, a little. Do, you like me?"

Danahlia's mouth opens but before she can speak, they hear another deep hiss from somewhere nearby. The Liguna rises from the mud, looking in the direction the sound came from, saying excitedly, "Ooo, that's another one. Let's go get it."

Alice frowns but follows.

Chapter 11

Weep for the Fishes

Alice peers through the grasses along the flooded river's shores to another of the large reptiles who looks to be warming itself in a patch of sunlight. Its dark green scaled hide looks very tough and bumpy, not smooth like Danahlia at all. Its tail is tapered and long, perhaps as long as it's ovular body, though the tail is more tall than wide, with ridges on top while being rounded along the sides. Four short legs poke out from the front and rear of the body, ending in small curved claws with webbing between its toes. But it's most arresting feature by far is its mouth. Long and thin, it ends in a bulge with nostril slits on top while a viciously impressive array of teeth juts out along the entire length.

Alice approaches the beast cautiously, constantly scanning the area for any more of the monstrous creatures. She has drawn her sword, and holds it just over the damp grasses, her slow footsteps squishing in the mud. Getting closer lets the young fox girl appreciate the size of the reptile and she begins to regret letting Danahlia talk her out of hitting it with a few arrows first. The Liguna had convinced her that doing so would only make the creature flee into the murky water where they'd dare not follow. This plan relied entirely on surprise.

Her quarry seems to be sleeping, it's breath slow and steady until it notices her. Perhaps scent or sound alerts the monster and it turns to her with an angry deep hiss, accompanied by an opening of its massive jaws. It's surprisingly clean, pink mouth offers no preparation for the horrid, warm stink of rotten flesh that rolls from it as it rumbles at the Tokala. Alice holds her sword low, waving it before the creature and it snaps at the weapon. Taking the reptile's full attention, it doesn't notice until too late Danahlia leaping at it from behind, her spear plunging cross brace deep into its skull. The menacing jaws fall shut as the creature immediately goes limp.

Danahlia slipped as she made her attack, ending with her sitting atop the creature, but she none the less whoops with joy, "Yeah! We can eat off him for days!"

The creature is incredibly heavy which, Danahlia is certain, means it has a lot of meat. They consider how to bring it back to camp, unable to carry the entire thing. Alice laments not having Twinkaleni around. The small mage could have used her earth magic to simply float the thing back. After discussion and then argument, Danahlia finally concedes to let Alice remove the head and clear out the organs. After hacking off the monster's tail, they discover how incredibly resilient the reptile's hide is and try flipping it over. The belly of the beast is not nearly so tough and after cutting it open, and letting it bleed out, they half dump half pull out the entrails. It's messy business, but without its insides and head, they can at least manage the weight.

Alice slings the thick, fleshy tail over her shoulder while Danahlia hoists up the body. She has trouble getting a good hold and ends up with it in an awkward hug, forcing her to take wide, waddling steps. Danahlia tries to get Alice to take the head too, wanting very much to show the others the vicious jaws the pair had had to overcome but Alice refuses, saying it's unnecessary weight. The walk to camp is slow and careful, the girls not wanting to encounter any more of the beasts while so burdened, but they do come up with a name for them. Sawtooths.

As they approach camp late that afternoon, Danahlia calls out, "Hey, Twinkie! Get the fire goin', we got dinner!"

The Murin is curious and pleased with their catch, commenting that it should sustain them for some time. When asked how they got it and why they're so dirty, Danahlia drops the carcass and tells her an entirely fabricated story of how she had heroically saved Alice from a monster who's jaws were at least as large as it's body and could not be brought due to their enormous weight and dangerous teeth. Twinkaleni has learned to ignore Danahlia's embellishments and doesn't bother inquiring further, instead telling the girls that she had come up with a way to weaken the wall and hopefully greatly speed its downfall.

Either pouting because Twinkaleni didn't like her story or simply because she's hungry, Danahlia wanders off to collect firewood. Meanwhile, Twinkaleni takes Alice to the wall to discuss her plan. The Murin explains that by setting and sustaining fires at various points in and along the wall, especially near the thicker root tendrils, the heat will eventually weaken the structural integrity of the barrier, making bringing it down that much easier. Alice likes the plan, as it seems far less labor intensive than actually ripping and cutting through the entire thing. Far too tired to enact it now, Alice retires to gathering sticks and branches for their cooking fire.

Already exhausted, skinning the sawtooth proves difficult, even with the giant ant mandibles the girl's had saved. The hide is thick and tough, particularly on top, like a natural armor. The girls have to resort to two handed swings of Alice's sword just to start spots to work in their smaller, more manageable tools. But they're happy to see that is does have a great deal of edible meat, fresh and lovely pink. As they cut free chunks, they place the larger ones directly on their fire while the smaller bits are skewered on sticks.

The scent of cooking meat seems to finally rouse Kaliska who was still sleeping when Alice and Danahlia had arrived. The Chitali groggily rises, sniffing the air and grimacing as she does.

Spotting the girls cooking and the carcass nearby, Kaliska bursts, "Wha-?! You killed something else?! WHY?! What is wrong with you?!"

As the deer girl stomps over to them, Alice calls, "Kali, calm down."

Though Danahlia, more angrily, shouts, "Whoa, we got this guy fair and square." She then recounts her tale of having to save Alice from nearly being eaten by the monster.

Alice doesn't care for her part as a helpless damsel in distress, but she figures the truth would only destabilize matters and goes along with it when a clearly agitated Kaliska looks to her for confirmation.

"And it would have been disrespectful to the sawtooth's sacrifice to just leave it there to rot," Alice decides to add.

Danahlia nods, "Exactly, we're showin' our appreciation for the river's loss by eatin' it and not lettin' it go to waste."

This seems to calm the deer girl some, but not much, and she immediately climbs the wall to make a loud prayer to the river god, being sure the others hear her apologize for their behavior and the loss of yet another life. The others shrug and continue cooking their dinner. When Kaliska climbs down, she stomps back into camp, glaring at the others before she plops down. Then she gets back up and has some of her tea, clearly intent on giving her companions the silent treatment. This turns out to be a nice respite from her constant shaming over animal cruelty.

The sawtooth meat is rather tough, requiring thorough chewing and small bites, but is warm and satisfying. It tastes vaguely like chicken though with its own unique, perhaps fishy, twist. The girls greatly enjoy it, or at least most of them do. Kaliska throws them dirty looks ever so often as she eats her stash of vegetarian fare. After they're sated, Danahlia stretched uncomfortably and asks the Chitali if she can heal her muscles as she had Alice's. Kaliska just frowns and looks away. After some begging, Danahlia is forced to give up, shambling in defeat back to the fire. Seeing this, Alice decides to offer her services as a masseuse.

The Tokala had never given a massage, rarely seen it done, and only ever received the magic infused one by Kaliska, but she feels she has the basic idea. She begins on Danahlia's arms, the Liguna saying they're the sorest. Danahlia sits smiling up at Alice gratefully as the fox girl, on her knees, rubs her smooth, firm, biceps. Danahlia moans her approval and tells Alice not to be shy about "really gettin' in there." Alice rubs harder, pushing the Liguna's muscles around like kneading dough. Danahlia groans loudly and then falls back, lifting her arms to purposely knock Alice over and pin her legs. The Liguna makes noises of exaggerated pleasure, wiggling up and on top of Alice, holding her down while Alice laughs, trying to push the larger girl off.

Once Danahlia shimmies her head onto Alice's chest, she stops and looks up at the Tokala, grinning widely. Alice meets her gaze, sharing her smile, but then Danahlia looks past her. Alice follows her sight to Twinkaleni, watching them with a somewhat curious expression.

Danahlia shimmies up closer and whispers, "Hey, Twinkie's real ticklish on her belly and feet, let's get 'er."

Alice grins and nods. Danahlia rolls off of her and they both walk nonchalantly in opposite directions while slowly approaching the small mouse girl.

Twinkaleni looks to them suspiciously but as they get further apart she is forced to focus on one, demanding of Alice, "What are you doing?"

Alice shrugs, her hands around her back, trying to suppress a grin, "Nothin'."

Twinkaleni narrows her eyes at her and tries to turn to Danahlia, but the Liguna is already upon her, taking both her tiny hands and lifting them over her head, shouting, "Go go go!"

Twinkaleni squeaks indignantly as Alice swiftly moves in, getting her hands under the mage's loose shirt to begin ruthlessly tickling her belly. Alice hadn't done much tickling before but Danahlia was right, even the slightest twiddling of her fingers over the Murin's soft fur has the mage unable to speak coherently.

Twinkaleni gasps, "What are, ha, no, sto-ah ahahaha!"

Encouraged, Alice roams over the Murin's stomach relentlessly and can't help but laugh herself, seeing Twinkaleni shake her head, jerking and giggling. The small mage hardly ever laughed, and never this hard. Kaliska joins in, taking hold of one of the Murin's kicking feet and flitters her fingers over the bottom of it. This inspires a new wave of laughs, squeaks, and even a cute little snort from the tiny girl. They don't stop until they're all laughing and Twinkaleni cries that she's about to wet herself, tears of mirth in her large amber eyes.

Joining them in tickle torture puts Kaliska in a better mood and they let Twinkaleni try to recover her dignity as Alice and Danahlia climb the wall to wash up. Now knowing of the sawtooths, the pair keeps to the water's edge, cleaning the dry mud from themselves the best they can. As they do, Alice finds herself sneaking glances at the Liguna, for some reason terribly fascinated by how the water weighs down her shirt, making it cling to the well-formed curves of her body. Danahlia faces away from her and bends over to spread water over her legs. Alice, under the guise of cleaning some mud from her shoulder, watches from the corner of her eye as Danahlia lifts her lengthy tail up and lets it curl a bit so it looks like a question mark floating over her. The next time the Tokala looks over at the rather enviable Liguna, she finds her staring right back, grinning upside down from between her thighs.

Alice starts a little, feeling her fur bristle with embarrassment as she quickly looks away, refocusing on her task. She can somehow feel Danahlia still watching her and refuses to look back, as doing so would only reveal further her spying. For a minute or two more, she focuses intently on getting clean until she feels wet hands gliding over her back, making her jump again. Alice looks over her shoulder to find Danahlia behind her, rubbing slowly and gently across her with both hands.

"What are you doing?" she asks.

"Mud back here too," Danahlia says simply, "I'll do yours and, if you ask nicely, I might just let you do mine."

Alice hears the smirk in the taller girl's tone and tosses back, "Oh, I'm not sure I'm worthy of such a privilege."

Danahlia gives her shoulders a little squeeze, "You'll do fine."

As Danahlia works, her hands begin to roam over to Alice's sides, around her flanks, and down her slender hips. Alice halts her own efforts to clean herself, unable to keep focused with the new attention. She inhales sharply as Danahlia's hands roam over her, slowly reaching around to her stomach with slow circular motions, a buzzing heat steadily building within her despite wet clothes and the shade of trees. Alice jumps again as Danahlia presses her chest to Alice's back and pulls her into a wonderfully comforting and strangely alarming embrace. The young fox girl's mind struggles between pulling away and letting herself be taken in. She chooses the later.

Alice forcibly releases the tension in her body, steadily relaxing into the larger girl, feeling her warmth even through both layers of damp clothing. Danahlia holds her closer, placing her chin atop the fox girl's head, a cheek to either ear. Alice decides she can't let Danahlia do all the work and reaches back to place her hands on both of the Liguna's smooth thighs. She gives them a little squeeze, feeling the firm muscle under her pants. Danahlia sighs contentedly and they begin to sway as if to some unheard music.

Alice finds herself making little pleased noises with every exhale as the pair enjoys the pleasure of each other's company. Danahlia lifts her head while slowly running a hand up Alice's stomach, over her chest, up her throat, and, with a finger, raises her chin so they can look into each other's eyes. Alice returns Danahlia's smile but just before they can join their lips, they hear Kaliska talking excitedly, her voice growing as she nears. They part immediately, turning away from each other and looking toward the chatter.

Kaliska and Twinkaleni are making their way toward them, the Chitali shouting, "She did it!" upon spotting the other pair.

As the excited deer girl bounds toward them, she singsongs, "She did it, she did it, she did it!"

"She did what?" Alice asks as Kaliska takes her by the hands and hops cheerily around making the fox girl spin in a circle.

Kaliska stops abruptly, turning to Alice, wide eyed, "The thing! The thing where she made the juice come out of a doogy, with her mind."

"You got that spell to work?" wonders Danahlia as the Murin joins them.

"I've managed to extract a few meager drops," the Murin mage admits, then smiles up at them, "but it is progress none the less."

Twinkaleni receives a round of congratulations and while the girls wash up a bit, Kaliska describes what she saw with animated gestures. Twinkaleni, carefully going through her light gray fur, reiterates the versatility of such a skill and feels confident that with proper mastery, it would no doubt aid the girls greatly in their travels. The others agree, and once their done washing, the party heads back to camp. There, they eagerly gather around to watch the mage perform her great feat once more.

Twinkaleni sits with her doogyak in her lap, focusing intently while making smoke like gestures with both tiny hands. Nothing happens. The girls sit quietly around, watching for even the slightest changes but after several minutes, Danahlia loses interest and wanders off to cook more sawtooth. Alice lingers a little longer but eventually the smell of flame seared meat takes her attention as well. Kaliska, having no interest in the flesh of dead things, stays the longest but even she tires after a while. Alice returns with a hunk of meat and settles in to watch while she eats. Kaliska eventually consents to healing Danahlia's still aching muscles when she is presented with the fact that she'd rather have Alice alive than the beast that, Danahlia insists, nearly ate her.

The fox girl is in the middle of tearing off another mouth full when she spots a tiny wisp of what looks like steam rising from Twinkaleni's doogyak. In the waning light of the evening, it's so faint she isn't sure she actually saw anything at all and looks closer. As she does, a bit more rises from the melon. The spindly wiggle of moisture looks so fragile that a light breath would be more than enough to blow it away, so Alice holds hers. As she watches, the wisp gains more body, fattening up as more mist like moisture joins it. It's strangely fascinating how much like steam it appears, but unlike steam, it doesn't rise and disperse. Alice can see it clearly now, the vapor gathering steadily, and lets her meat hang from her mouth so she can turn to wave frantically to the others, not wanting to risk her voice costing Twinkaleni precious focus.

Danahlia looks up, "What? She doin' it?"

The Tokala puts a finger over her meat filled mouth and waves them over more frantically with one hand. They join her, silently watching the wisp gain substance until is coalesces into several tiny drops of water. Twinkaleni's eyes open for the first time since she started, her hands reaching around the drops as if holding an invisible ball containing them. The drops form into a single large drop and she smiles at her apparently exhausting work.

It is quite obvious that any one of them could have gotten substantially more liquid from the melon if they simply squeezed it but the girls give the Murin mage this victory and cheer her accomplishment. Now that the water is free, Twinkaleni has no problems manipulating it in the air and has it hover over her palms so her companions can plainly see it.

That is until Danahlia leans in, sticks out her pink fleshy tongue, and laps it up.
"Mmm, not bad Twinkie," the Liguna comments approvingly.

Alice watches Twinkaleni's eyes go wide and her mouth open in disbelief, but instead of raising a fuss, she flops back on the ground in exhaustion and begins to nibble on her melon.

Alice gives the Liguna a pointed look and Danahlia tilts her head, "What? She made it so we could drink it." Danahlia then frowns and gets Kaliska to follow her back to the fire, the Chitali eager to know what the magic water tasted like.

Alice turns away from them and offers Twinkaleni the hunk of meat she'd cooked. The little Murin accepts it with a slight nod, large amber eyes looking straight up. She hugs her food to her chest and interchangeably nibbles from both before pointing skyward. Alice looks to the canopy to find the light sprites have returned, their bluish white glows strengthening as the day ends. She decides to lie beside the tired mouse girl and watch the lights with her. They appear to be excitedly moving about the branches, clumping up in places while a few stragglers hurry to find groups, lights blinking at various intervals.

After a few minutes, many disappear above their branches, though Alice knows they're still there because of their lights reflecting off the leaves. A few more minutes pass and she asks Twinkaleni what she thinks they're doing. The mage doesn't answer, having fallen asleep at some point, her small arms loosely wrapped around her hunk of meat and melon. Alice smiles, continuing her vigil.

Eventually, a doogyak rolls off a tree branch just overhead. Instinctively, Alice holds up her open hands before her face, shutting her eyes and looking away. When nothing happens, she peers up to find the melon dangling in midair. It spins slowly as it gets steadily bigger and she realizes it's being lowered. She gets to her feet and reaches for it, waiting a few more inches until its weight rests in her open palm. Far too small to see but identifiable by the glowing bauble on its head, a light sprite looks over the branch and blinks several times.

Alice calls up quietly, as not to disturb the sleeping mage, "Are you givin' these to us?"

Several other sprites join the first, blinking off rhythm. Alice takes this to mean they are and plucks the thick web line free from the melon with a thank you. The sprites leave the web line, now free of its burden, right where it is and scatter about. Several more doogyaks are lowered and left for the girls.

Danahlia gives one she plucks a shake, "Why do they keep givin' us these things? There're loads of other fruits around."

"Probably because we keep eatin' 'em," says Kaliska, a half-eaten melon in either hand.

Over the next several days, the girls put Twinkaleni's plan into action. They create several small fires where she directs, the Murin claiming these select spots will do the most structural damage to the sour squirt dam. Kaliska had named the root tendril plant "sour squirts" after their pods and the name stuck. Much of these days are spent gathering whatever fallen wood can be found to maintain the fires. These fires are shoved deep within the wall, the idea being that as the roots around the fires dry out, they can add to the destruction, creating a chain reaction. Twinkaleni occasionally uses her magic to blow great gusts of wind into the hot spots, calling forth a bellowing inferno for a time, and very steadily, their sliver of the wall gets thinner and thinner.

Eventually their efforts are rewarded with a massive crack, that send them excitedly scurrying up the river's banks. Several more loud cracks have jets of water bursting through the weakened portion of the wall, their carefully tended fires dying in loud sizzles and sending up great plumes of steam. Still the wall holds. After several uneventful minutes, the party climbs up the wall, well to the side of the river, and watches, their excitement turning to frustration.

"What do we do now?" asks Kaliska.

The others have no answers. Twinkaleni begins to pace, one hand rubbing one of her great, round ears. Kaliska starts to follow the Murin, taking both ears in her hands and massaging them while Alice and Danahlia inspect the dam. The water had begun pushing the wall out so that now both sides were at an angle, but it seems to have caught itself and refuses to make way any further. With water seeping over and gushing through it, more fires would be impossible.

"Maybe if we wait, the water 'll push through," offers Alice, tired from their days of labor.

Danahlia frowns, her shoulders slumping, "Who knows how long that'll take and I'm tired o' waitin' around here. Let's just say we did it and go already."

After a few more moment's thought, Twinkaleni announces, "I have an idea. Everyone, step away from the dam."

The girls gather behind the mage and she calls, "Pavata!" while raising her hands off to her left, fingers splayed and flexing. Some of the water nearest the dam recedes into a decent sized wave.

Twinkaleni then throws her hands to her right and, like a puppet on strings, the wave follows her movements, battering the sour squirt wall. The jets of water spraying free from the dam intensify briefly and more cracks are heard.

"Yeah! Do it Twinkie!" cheers Danahlia, as Twinkaleni pulls her hands to the left once more, her movements strained as she creates an even larger wave.

"You can do it!" cries Alice.

Kaliska leaps into the air, pumping a fist, "Free the fishies!"

The mage sends the next wave smashing into the dam like a ram. Much of it flows over, but even more cracks are heard and a few more jets spray free. Her friends cheering her on, Twinkaleni musters one last wave, even larger than the previous. She sends it charging into the wall with such force that she falls, spinning to the ground, almost completely spent. The wave crashes into the stubborn dam, sending water splashing over the girls even several yards away.

The wall crackles some more, but holds.

The others help the small girl to her feet, Danahlia asking, "Got another one in ya?"

Twinkaleni is breathing heavily and has to be propped up just to stand. Even so, she looks to the wall with determination and raises her hands once more. But before she can gather her flagging energy, the wall groans loudly and with a final thunderous series of cracks, the dam gives, releasing the river at last.

The girls cheer, Kaliska raising Twinkaleni's limp arms so she can join in too. For a while, they sit to rest, watching the waters reclaim their bed with satisfaction. It's in the afternoon when this happens but even so, among the trees that overlook the river, light sprites begin to twinkle as far down the waterway as they can see.

The tired little party looks on for a time, the light sprites pulsating in what they take to be a grateful way. Then Alice notices the steadily draining flooded area revealing a bounty of aquatic life. Things big and small, too slow or perhaps too stubborn to be bothered by the retreating waters are left confused, shifting about in the thick mud left behind.

Turtles, frogs, a sawtooth that swiftly makes for the water, and things Alice doesn't recognize, are all left wandering. But more, there are loads of flopping- "Fish!" Alice calls, pointing. Dozens of them are scattered over the newly accessible area. Needing no further encouragement, the girls race to those nearest.

Alice reaches her first, picking it up by the tail to swing it around with the intent of slamming it against a rock to end its gasping. Kaliska screams for her to stop, giving the fox girl pause. Alice only has time to see Kaliska flying at her from behind before the Chitali's weight has her tumbling over face first into the mud. Nose aching, she rolls over the second she feels Kaliska's weight shift off of her and tries to yell angrily only to spit gritty gunk from her mouth while wiping at her stinging eyes. Alice clears her vision in time to see the deer girl release her fish into the river.

Immediately, Kaliska turns and charges at Danahlia, demanding she let her two fish go. Seeing what she did to Alice, Danahlia evades the Chitali's charge, by fainting to one side, then spinning away to the other. Even so, as Danahlia turns to flee, Kaliska grabs her by the tail and they both jerk forward, falling to the ground. Kaliska crawls over

Danahlia's back and tries to wrench the fish from her hands.

"Are you crazy? Get off o' me!" Danahlia sputters through the mud.

"Let them go!" screams Kaliska, when her finger strength proves weaker than the Liguna's.

"No, there mine!" insists Danahlia, trying to tuck the panicking fish closer to her body.

"Kali, stop it!" Alice shouts regaining her feet and running toward them.

In the struggle, Danahlia cries, "Agh! She's bitin' me!"

Alice closes on them and pushes Kaliska off. The Chitali has managed to free a fish and immediately sprints for the receding waters of the river. Enraged, Danahlia bursts from the ground, leaving her other fish flopping in the mud. Her angry feet kick up globs of muck as she closes on the deer girl and shoulder charges into her back so hard Kaliska somersaults forward in the wet earth, her hooves flailing through the air. Kaliska tumbles to a stop, covered with mud, as Danahlia seethes, lumbering toward her.

Alice steps between them, "Stop!"

The fury in Danahlia's eyes finds her and the Liguna growls, "She freakin' bit me! She's crazy! She *needs* to go!"

"Calm down, Danny," Alice pleads as Kaliska crawls toward the fish that fell from her grasp when she was knocked down. It lies still now.

Danahlia tries to push past her, "No! She's crazy! She's gonna get us killed out here! We need to cut her loose."

"We can't just leave her," claims Alice, the Liguna's efforts weakening.

"You want death so bad, then TAKE IT!" screams Kaliska, through what sounds like tears.

Danahlia jerks and Alice looks to see that she's caught the now dead fish Kaliska had been trying to save. Alice turns to the Chitali, who limps toward another flopping fish, one of her hands tucked in close to her chest.

Alice leaves Danahlia with her fish and runs to Kaliska, "Are you ok?"

"Help it!" Kaliska cries, pointing to another weakly flopping fish with her good hand, while she kneels to pick up the one at her hooves.

Alice looks between them and then puts a hand on Kaliska's arm, "You're hurt, let me-"

Kaliska roughly knocks into the Tokala with her shoulder and continues toward the river with her fish, "No! Help it!" She points back to the wiggling fish again, this time with her tucked hand, a motion that clearly pains her.

Alice looks back to Danahlia, who scowls and then turns away, she then looks to Twinkaleni, who hasn't yet moved from the spot she sits at and only watches from a distance, ears perked with interest. Not particularly sure why, Alice takes up the distraught deer girl's cause and begins picking up the still living fish, placing them carefully in the river.

They get many, but more than a few don't survive. Danahlia and Alice collect these. They would usually be ecstatic over the sudden abundance of food, but seeing Kaliska in the mud, hunched protectively over one of the dead fish while crying and trying desperately to massage it back to life kills the mood. As the pair bring their haul back to Twinkaleni, Danahlia examines her forearm. Alice can see a small ring of teeth marks with trails of dark red where blood had dripped from them.

"Are you ok?" asks Alice.

"Deer Nuts bit me. She keeps messin' up our hunts, freakin' out whenever we actually *do* catch something, *and* she's crazy," Danalia lets her bitten arm fall, "We gotta get rid of 'er. She's a liability."

She says this close enough to Twinkaleni that the Murin answers, still sitting in the grass, "She can also be an asset."

"Yeah, she can heal, when she *wants* to. Not worth it if you ask me," Danahlia grumbles.

"She can be helpful sometimes," says Alice.

Twinkaleni raises her chin, "I believe her true worth is yet revealed."

Danahlia drops her fish in the grass and then plops down on her rump to begin licking her wound. In between licks, she asks, "Worth?"

"Healing magic is often considered a gift from the gods. Those with this talent are highly valued. As we saw in Fiske, people are very eager to know and have healers around," Twinkaleni explains, "By having her with us, we would undoubtedly be granted favor in any settlement we happen across. This would significantly improve our ventures into populated areas, though at a cost."

"What cost?" asks Alice, joining her friends in the grass while looking over to the weeping Chitali.

Twinkaleni rubs at one of her ears, "Word of our passing would linger anywhere we go. It would make it that much easier for our enemies to-"

"Welp, that settles it then, we leave her," interrupts Danahlia.

"We can't just leave 'er," Alice interjects.

"Sure we can," the Liguna assures, "If she really does have a goddess or ghost or whatever watchin' out, I'm sure she'll be just fine."

"As I was about to point out," squeaks Twinkaleni, "The risk of leaving a trail for those who would seek us can be negated with proper precaution. And so I believe she would be more an asset than a hindrance, despite her... erratic tendencies." She says the last fiddling a few fingers at Kaliska.

Danahlia doesn't look up from her bite, "Fine, one vote for leave her, one vote for keep. You're the tie breaker, Fur Face."

"We can't just-" Alice starts, but a plopping noise makes her look to see a new dead fish settling on the girl's pile, Kaliska standing over it.

The Chitali gives them all a sour look through her mud caked face, thin trails of fur just under her eyes revealing the tread of tears, "We did this. We killed them all."

"Kali, we didn't know this would happen," insists Alice.

Kaliska spits back, "But you're happy about it."

"Bet your fuzzy little butt, Deer Nuts. We earned these," Danahlia gestures to the pile.

"They didn't have to die!" shouts Kaliska.

Danahlia starts to rise in anger, but Twinkaleni puts a hand on her leg, "We had little to do with their demise. They were too slow and weak to reach the river. Their stronger, faster kin were spared, and now enjoy their home as it was before the sour squirt dam came to be. This was our doing."

"Yeah, we probably saved way more than we took," nods Alice, "Now that the fish have the river back, they won't be so easy for the sawtooths to get at."

"These are the river god's way of sayin' thanks for all our hard work," claims Danahlia.

Kaliska frowns at the pile of dead fish, "They didn't have to die. We could have saved them. And I don't like your river god."

Danahlia huffs, "He probably doesn't like you either, seein' as you keep spittin' on his gifts," before going back to licking her wound.

Kaliska's frown deepens and she looks to the river for a moment before offering, "I'm sorry I bit you, but you really shouldn't kill things unless you need to."

Danahlia pauses to grumble, "So eatin' isn't a need for you is it? That must be nice."

Kaliska's lower lip trembles some but she stands her ground, "Let me heal that, then I'll go."

"Kali, no," pleads Alice.

But Danahlia tugs at her wrist, "That a promise?"

Kaliska gives a single nod and the Liguna offers her wounded arm. The Chitali tries to clap her hands, but it's clear her wrist or elbow is still bothering her. She then rubs her hands together, though without the vigor she usually puts into it, and then lays them over the bite marks she left in Danahlia. She hisses, looking at the damaged skin, and then the flesh begins to mend. When Kaliska's hands fall away, it's completely healed.

"Thanks," grumbles Danahlia, inspecting the healer's work.

Kaliska turns from them and begins limping down river.

Alice tries again, "Kaliska, wait, at least until-"

But Danahlia interrupts, "Let 'er go, Alice. She'll be better off in Fiske or someplace. She wasn't meant for adventures."

Alice begins to feel the burn of tears in her eyes and looks to Twinkaleni, who peers after the deer girl while maintaining silence. Alice rises, grabbing Kaliska's basket from where it lay in a pile with the rest of their things and begins after her. Danahlia grabs her by the foot, but she snarls back at her, bearing her teeth, and kicks free.

It's not difficult to catch up to the limping Chitali, and Alice says to her, "Kali, Kali, we voted. You can stay with us."

Kaliska continues on without even a glance at the Tokala, "Nope."

"Why?" Alice demands, and when she doesn't get a reply she goes on, "Kali, please, you can't go all the way back on your own, you're hurt. At least heal yourself first."

"Nope," is all she gets.

"Kali, please," Alice cries, "You won't make it back all the way to Fiske on your own."

"Will to. Althea will guide me," she says stubbornly, raising her chin, and then nearly falls because she can't see where she's placing her hooves.

"Then at least take your basket, to remember us by," Alice insists, holding it out to her.

Kaliska sighs and stops, accepting the basket and placing it on her back. Alice uses the opportunity to plead with her some more until Kaliska finally says, "Althea said I'm supposed to help people. If I go with you guys, I'll only help three. But if I go back to Fiske, I can help more."

"But we'll go to other places, other towns, villages, you can help them too," assures Alice.

"Maybe, but there aren't that many people further north. I wanna help lots of people, so I'm going south, and maybe west, or east, or even south some more. Good-bye Alice, and may Althea watch over you too." With that, the mud covered Chitali heads off once more.

Alice gives a defeated wave and watches her go, "Bye... Kali."

Chapter 12

The Cave

Alice shuffles her way back to her remaining friends. Danahlia is by the river washing up while Twinkaleni is gathering twigs for a fire. Alice decides to clean herself off as well, though she does so with her back to the Liguna, some distance from her. In the middle, she feels a splash of water on her and looks over to see Danahlia has moved considerably closer but washes as if unaware. Alice ignores her, shin deep in water, and continues her efforts to extract the dried mud from her fur. A bigger splash hits her lower back and she turns to see Danahlia only feet away now, grinning. Alice refuses to acknowledge her any more than that, blaming her for Kaliska leaving the group.

Danahlia's tail pokes around at Alice's back and she slaps it away, "Stop."

The Liguna frowns, "Look, it sucks but not everyone is gonna fit in with us. You can't be mad at me for that."

"You're the reason Kali left! You called her names and hurt her and just made her feel so unwelcome!" Alice fires back.

Danahlia raises her arms, "Whoa, are you just gonna ignore the fact that she bit me?!"

"She was tryin' to save the fish!" Alice gestures to the water.

"Yeah, fish! We eat fish! Don't deny it. You would have no problem takin' all we could if she wasn't there to guilt trip us."

"And you hurt her, she was limping when she left!"

"Uh, again, she bit me," exclaims Danahlia, showing her own teeth, "She shouldn't've started somethin' she couldn't finish."

"What if she doesn't make it back to Fiske? She's hurt and alone and she doesn't know how to survive out here." As the words leave her lips, Alice feels tears begin to well in her eyes again.

"She was fine before we met, she'll be fine now," Danahlia assures.

Twinkaleni decides to remind them that, "She was passed out in the dirt and nearly dead from dehydration when we met her."

"But that won't be a problem now, will it?" asks Danahlia with a wave down the river, "Guys, you're not seein' the bigger picture here. She wanted us to stop eatin' meat. Meat! Do you have any idea what would happen if I stopped eatin' meat completely?" Before the others can say anything Danahlia bursts, "I don't know, because I've never been crazy enough to try it! That's probably what's wrong with her, no meat. Got her head all messed up." She fiddles a few clawed fingers beside her own head for emphasis. Alice turns away, no longer interested in discussing things. She hears Danahlia sigh behind her, "She'll be fine. Deer Nuts probably already healed herself and is stridin' back to Fiske with that weird sense of purpose she has."

"Don't call her that," Alice says pointedly, resuming her bath.

Dinner is a fairly silent affair with only a brief discussion on their next course of action. The girls decide to follow the river to wherever it leads, hopefully deep into the mountain. This way they have a ready source of food and water while they make their way through it. That night, for the first time in a while, Alice doesn't sleep beside Danahlia. Kaliska had the tarp in her basket so they don't even have it to keep them together. Instead, they lay scattered on the ground.

A trio once more, the girls follow along the river the best they can for several days. Rough uphill terrain and thick brush force them to take the occasional detour but they always find their way back to the river. With Twinkaleni's growing mastery of water magic, the party is never left wanting for fish and the time steadily mends the rift that had formed between Alice and Danahlia. Eventually, their journey leads to an imposing cliff and a majestic waterfall.

Cascading down, perhaps a hundred feet or more from a sheer rocky outcropping, is crystal clear water, made white when splashing on gray, weather worn stone. All along the fall are plants clinging to the rocks, taking in the dense mist shed from the tumbling waters. Below, spread before the three, is a wide plunge pool, messily engulfing the endless falling water. A deep fog covers the pool and cools Alice's fur as she and her friends approach. The forest is especially lush around the shore and many small things go unseen as they scurry into the water, adding their own ripples to the constantly undulating surface. The mid-day sun breaks through the trees here, giving the surface of the pool a white and gold glow.

"Wow," says Alice in awe, having never seen a waterfall before.

"Last one in gets the fire wood!" exclaims Danahlia racing to the shore, tossing off her back pack along with her clothes.

The last few days hike have Alice ready for a break and she swiftly joins the Liguna, getting down to her bare fur. The water is wonderfully cold, soothing her aching feet, as she splashes in. Danahlia dives, disappearing under the surface, her long tail slithering behind her. Alice treads until the water is thigh deep and then plops down into the soft muddy bottom, a shiver running through her as the cold water saps her body heat. She lets out a sigh and leans back, letting her arms, legs, and tail relax, floating with the current. She looks for Danahlia but sees no sign of her and then looks to Twinkaleni. The Murin sits on the shore with only her feet in the water, tiny pink toes wiggling just at the surface. Alice smiles at her and gets a smile back.

Alice eventually spots Danahlia emerging along the far shore. She's stooped over and appears to be chasing something greenish and squat fleeing up the beach. It makes a mad dash for the bushes, disappearing among them. After looking around, Danahlia gives up the chase, turning to Alice and putting up an index finger and thumb to show just how close she was to catching it. Alice grins and waves her back over. Danahlia is heading back into the water when a horrible noise can be heard over even the constant roar of the waterfall. Danahlia ducks from it as if anticipating a blow and then turns to the bushes where the small creature had run. A massive monster stomps into view.

Comparing it to Danahlia, who leaps into the water and begins swimming hurriedly away, the creature is even larger than a shatterhead command-boar. Its back glitters in the light with dazzling greens, making Alice think it probably has scales. She can only make out basic features at this distance but it's clear it has four stumpy legs, a thick rounded body, and ends in a wide tapering tail. It's head seems to fan out near the back giving it's face an angular arrowhead like look, save for the single large horn jutting up just over its nose. It opens its mouth at Danahlia, revealing it to be beak-like, and lets loose another furious, high pitched cry.

For a terrifying few seconds, Alice simply watches as the creature plunges into the pool after the Liguna. Danahlia is a fast swimmer but the shallow water allows the creature to simply run through, its angular head held low to let it cut through the water like the prow of a ship. Once its tail is submerged, it trashes wildly, lending the creature greater speed. Alice waves frantically for Danahlia to head in her direction and then thinks, *what am I gonna do when it gets here?* Immediately she splashes to the shore to where her bow and arrows lie, near where Twinkaleni is standing, watching with wide, amber eyes.

Bare furred and dripping wet, Alice gathers up her bow and arrows, asking frantically, "What is that thing?!"

Twinkaleni stutters, "Uh, I believe, that is a Tiposaur. The, um, book had a... an entry."

"What did it say? How do you kill it?" demands Alice, taking a few of her arrows and jamming them point first into the ground while she kneels behind them to nock one in her bow.

"It's, so big," says Twinkaleni in awe.

"Twinkaleni! Where's it weak?!" shouts Alice, taking aim at the massive creature chasing after her desperately swimming friend.

The mouse mage jolts from her staring and says, "Armored head and hide. I can do little with Danahlia in the way."

Alice pulls back, wondering where to target and then centers on its eyes. She looses an arrow and watches as it bounces off the flared head of the creature, doing nothing.

Alice fires several more shots with similar results until Twinkaleni shouts beside her, "Dive! Dive!" then to Alice she says, "I can't get a clear shot, she must go under."

Alice nods her understanding and begins to shout with her to Danahlia, "Dive! Dive!" She pushes down at the air trying to convey the message to the Liguna, still a ways off.

Danahlia gets it, lifts up out of the water and then slips under.

The moment her tail disappears, Twinkaleni shouts, "Feasta!" sending a stream of fire flowing from her hands and at the monster.

The creature seems aware of the mage's attack and submerges its head, the fire pouring over its flared part and back, not slowing at all. The small mage ceases her attack to examine its effect. The moment her fire stops, the tiposaur's large head rises just as it belches a burst of water with a powerful puff of sound. Alice only has time to turn away and duck before she feels the moisture of the water shot whoosh past her, punching a hole through a bush further up the shore.

Alice and Twinkaleni survey the broken branches and then look to each other in surprise before taking cover behind some rocks and a tree. Twinkaleni launches several more gouts of flame as Alice scans the water, searching for Danahlia in between arrows. Another blast of water smashes into the tree Twinkaleni hides behind. It hits with such force that chunks of bark fly off on impact. Under the girl's ranged assaults, the tiposaur seems hesitant to leave the safety of the deeper water and circles a bit before retreating back to the opposite shore, arrows and flames lapping at its flank.

Alice slumps in relief as she watches the creature climb onto the far bank and lumber back into the bushes, her supply of arrows nearly spent. Twinkaleni falls to her bottom, taking in deep breathes, the battle having cost her as well. Danahlia eventually pops up on shore nearby, looks around cautiously, and then makes her way to the others.

Breathing hard she asks, "Geez, what got that one all riled up?"

Twinkaleni points an accusing little pink finger at the tallest girl, "You," she huffs, "were chasing its young."

Danahlia gives her a negligent wave, "Psh. What was that thing anyway?"

"Twinklaeni says it's a tiposaur," informs Alice, then she asks the Murin, "Are those things always so aggressive? It might be dangerous to stay around here. What if there's more of 'em?"

Twinkaleni replies, "The book says, they are generally very docile," she then narrows her eyes at Danahlia, "as long as they or their young are not threatened."

"See," shrugs the Liguna, "I didn't know that. Besides, we showed 'em."

"Me and Twinkaleni showed 'em. You were busy runnin' away," says Alice.

Danahlia purses her lips and raises her chin, "Runnin' away, or baitin' it?"

"Running away," asserts both Alice and Twinkaleni together.

"Swimming away," Danahlia corrects.

Twinkaleni lifts a hand with a shake of her head, "Regardless, it may be wise to seek a more secure location. Who knows what else lurks about here, especially after dark."

Tired, Alice pouts, "But we just got here."

Danahlia nods, "Yeah, come on Twinkie, we've been on the move for days, let's just relax a little."

Twinkaleni raises her small hands, "I don't mean we leave the waterfall. I mean we should look for a more defensible position nearby before it becomes too dark to do so, unless of course you want to sleep out in the open with creatures of that size stomping about."

"Oh, yeah," says Danahlia pointing by the falls, "I think I saw some caves over there."

The caves she thought she saw mostly turn out to be shallow dimples in the rocks, though almost directly behind the falls, Alice finds a real one. The cave is taller than it is wide, tall enough that even standing on Danahlia's shoulders Alice doubts she could reach the top, and wide enough that all three of them can walk side by side. The walls of the cave are rounded, Twinkaleni surmises, unnaturally so. Sunlight fails a few yards in so Twinkaleni sends a little ball of evening orange light down the cave to reveal that it is rather deep. They spend some time shouting down the cavern, hearing their voices echo off the stone, in an attempt to lure anything within out into the open. When nothing is forth coming, the girls prepare their weapons and head in.

Alice and Danahlia walk beside one another while Twinkaleni takes up the rear and holds the light. The rock is cold and unyielding underfoot. Bugs and other things skitter away from their approach but nothing impressive emerges from the surrounding shadows. Alice's ears angle at every sound, though the loudest are their own footsteps echoing in the dark. Water drips from somewhere above onto Alice's head. She pulls her ears back and tries to avoid it, only for another drop to land on her nose. The cave has a few gradual turns, but remains the same size for the most part. Occasionally, Twinkaleni will send out her little ball of light floating ahead of them and they stop to watch what it reveals. So far, only more rock and a few puddles.

The cave goes on for what feels like hours, but is likely less than one as the girls' pace is cautiously slow. To conserve her energy, Twinkaleni dims her light and takes the lead. After a time walking this way, Alice smells something foul, like rotten eggs.

"Ugh, geez, Twinkie. You need to warn people before you go blastin' off like that. We're right behind you," exclaims Danahlia, her voice echoing back distorted.

Twinkaleni narrows her eyes back at her and whispers, "It was not me. Perhaps it is the scent of whatever occupies this cave, and thanks to you, it may now be aware of our presence."

Alice shushes them both, listening carefully and hearing something just under the girl's chatter.

They listen for a minute before Danahlia giggles, "Stinky Twinkie."

Alice tries to hold back a laugh, her cheeks puffing out, but the more she does the more it bubbles up until she lets out a little sputtering bark that echoes around them.

This sets Danahlia off laughing until Twinkaleni smacks her in the thigh with a, "Shhh!"

Danahlia shushes her back with a poke to her forehead. The light goes out and the Liguna yelps. Alice shushes them again more harshly, feeling the two begin to tussle.

"You shush, she bit me. Why do people keep biting me?" complains Danahlia, shoving a hand at Alice.

Alice shoves back and gets another harder shove in return. Twinkaleni squeaks in pain somewhere in the dark and Alice feels around for Danahlia's arm, grabs it, and opens her mouth to bite. But then they hear a harsh burst of noise echo through the cave and freeze. More noise follows, like a constant murmur, but the acoustics in the cave make it impossible to tell from what direction it's coming.

"Oh ticks," mutters Alice, "What's that?"

"Which ways it comin' from?" asks Danahlia, moving about uncertainly.

"Calm down the both of you," Twinkaleni says shakily, then in a much quitter tone she goes on, "If that is some sort of speech, it is possible whatever is making it may be intelligent and may not be alone."

Hearing this makes Alice distinctly uncomfortable, the oppressive darkness not helping in the least. The murmurs go on and Alice begins to feel herself shake as she whispers, "You think there's more than one?"

"It is a possibility we should be aware of," Twinkaleni whispers back from somewhere else.

Danahlia grabs hold of Alice by the arm, her voice quavering, "Oh ticks, I am way too young and pretty to be turned into cave monster poop."

"Shhh, I have a plan, but we *must* determine from which direction the sound approaches from," says Twinkaleni.

"What're you gonna do?" asks Alice, peering around in the blackness, her sword held tight, the blade low and against the cave wall.

"Once we determine the direction, I can send a wave of fire down the tunnel. Mind you, the cold stone around us will greatly limit the amount of heat I can gather," explains Twinkaleni, "But it may be enough to make it or them think twice before continuing this way."

"What if it just makes it angry?" asks Danahlia, squeezing Alice's arm tighter, her hand shaking nervously.

Twinkaleni takes in a breath, "If it comes to an engagement, I'll have to rely on the two of you. I will try to maintain a light so you may at least see our foe."

"Great," murmurs Danahlia, "whose idea was it to check in here again?"

"Yours," mumbles Alice, taking hold of Danahlia's wrist.

Danahlia sighs, "Well ok, fine. If we don't make it out of here, I'm sorry I got us eaten."

Alice gives the Liguna a squeeze and the harsh burst of sound comes again, even louder. The girls jump at the noise and then stand as still as they can, hearing the echo bounce through the large tunnel. The murmuring continues after and Alice feels like she can make out the pauses in between the words, but not the words themselves.

"Which way?" whispers Twinkaleni.

"I, that way, I think," stutters Alice, pointing.

"Which?" asks Twinkaleni.

Danahlia shift in the darkness and Alice refuses to let go of her arm, "This way, aim this way."

Alice feels along Danahlia's smooth fingers to Twinkaleni's soft furred head, the Murin now standing before them. The others' shaking gives her some small comfort as her mind creates images of horrible things lurking in the shadows. Alice desperately pushes these aside, steeling herself and readying her sword. She feels Danahlia beside her shift with her spear, the Liguna's tail wrapping around to run along Alice's leg for assurance.

The muttering is louder now, definitely words, but distorted and unintelligible among its own eerie echoes.

"Hit 'em hard, Twinkie, and then step back behind us," instructs Danahlia in a barely audible tone.

Alice feels the air chill considerably all of a sudden, no breeze, just a swift drop in temperature as Twinkaleni gather's all the available heat for her spell. The muttering stops, perhaps the creature feeling the change as well. And then a familiar goose-like honk of a sneeze sounds from somewhere nearby, echoing loudly.

"Kaliska?" Alice calls to the darkness.

Silence for a moment, then, "Althea? Is that you? Are you sure this is the right way?"

The girls let out a collective sigh of relief, "No, it's Alice."

"Yeah, where's Alice? Is she in here?" Kaliska calls back from even closer.

"Kali, it's us," says Danahlia

Twinkaleni lets out a breath, warm heat radiating out from her as she summons up a tiny speck of light. It's blinding after the pitch blackness but when Alice can see again, she finds the Chitali standing before them, her hands raised over her face to shield her eyes.

"Kali!" she cries, running up to give the deer girl a hug, and finding that she's wet for some reason.

Kaliska jumps at the touch but then embraces it, feeling all over the Tokala, "Oh, Alice, it's you! I'm so glad I finally found you."

"We thought you were a freakin' monster, what are you doin' here?" exclaims Danahlia, stepping up to wrap her arms around both girls.

Kaliska tells them that shortly after she left for Fiske, the Goddess Althea spoke to her and was not happy at all that she left Alice's company. Kaliska had tried to reason that by going back she could help more people but the goddess wouldn't hear of it and demanded she return to the trio, insisting she would do more with them.

"I asked how, but she got upset and left again," Kaliska says with lowered ears and a frown.

"How did you find us?" wonders Twinkaleni.

"Why are you all wet?" asks Alice.

"The water fall, I thought I saw Althea in it, but it was just water. Then I saw your foot prints," Kaliska says, pointing to her own hooves.

The girls decide to continue on their effort to secure the cave, still uncertain if anything dwells within. Far more relaxed now, they move with hurried purpose as Kaliska tells them of her conversation with the supposed goddess. When Danahlia asks about how she plans to get along with meat eaters, Kaliska says that Althea told her that gaining sustenance from others is an essential part of life for *some* beings and is not to be condemned as long as the killing is for survival.

"Yeah, remember that Kali, you said it yourself, *essential*," says Danahlia.

Kaliska crosses her arms and frowns at the Liguna, "She said I don't have to like it, just accept it and to keep it warm."

"Keep what warm?" asks Alice.

"I don't know," Kaliska shrugs. She sneezes again and then smiles, "Maybe our friendship."

Alice grins too, glad to have her back. The party makes their way through the dark, Twinkaleni leading with her tiny ball of light. As they press on, the coldness of the stone chilled air seems to get steadily warmer, which doesn't help the rotten egg smell at all.

"Ugh, it's gettin' worse. Let's head back, nothin's down here," says Danahlia, holding a thumb and index finger over her nostril slits.

Alice is about to agree when Twinkaleni announces, "I feel something ahead, I believe we are almost at the end."

With some disgruntled mumbling the girls continue forward.

The light around the Murin changes, no longer reflecting off the walls or ceiling and after a few feet more, Alice feels why. Though she can't see it, the air feels less confined here. It's warm also, more than it was. Twinkaleni strengthens her tiny ball of light and sends it flying out at an upward angle. It takes some time for the light to reflect off the ceiling and then puff out, revealing that they have entered a massive underground chamber of some sort. Before Twinkaleni can summon up another light, the walls and floor begin to shimmer faintly as if the stone has the last dying embers of a fire sprinkled over it.

They all stand in awe as the chamber glows around them, not bright by any means but enough to at least make out the silhouettes of stones and see just how massive a chamber they've stumbled into. Alice reaches for the faint embers on an outcropping of rock beside her and feels the subtle warmth radiating off the surface even before she touches it. It's rough like any other rock, but warm, as if it had only recently been sitting in the sun.

"Wow, what is this stuff?" wonders Danahlia, picking up a glowing stone.

"It's so pretty," says Kaliska, her silhouette spinning in a slow circle.

Alice notices more substantial pockets of light further away and asks, "Is this magic?"

Twinkaleni takes in a deeply satisfied breath, "Oh yes. There is great power here, I can feel it." The tiny Murin starts toward the larger concentrations of ember light, breathing deeply despite the smell.

"Hey, hold on, Mini-Mage, what is this stuff?" Danahlia asks, holding up her glowing rock as the others hurriedly follow the tiny mouse girl.

"I believe this substance is known as emberstone," Twinkaleni says dreamily, working up to a jog.

"What's emberstone?" asks Alice, walking quickly but carefully, not wanting to stub a toe.

"It is one of many resulting substances that can occur when magical energy is present in a location for an extended period of time. It, fuses with what is around it, resulting in natural magical formations such as this," the Murin explains, hurrying to the greater glow near the center of the chamber.

As the four approach it, the heat intensifies, even under foot. It's not hot, but it is noticeable.

"Who knew stone could be so warm," says Kaliska, brushing a hand over various glowing bits of the emberstone as she passes.

"Is this stuff valuable?" asks Danahlia.

Twinkaleni seems too enamored to answer, so Alice tells her, "Probably. It's like magic everyone can use."

"Hey, yeah. Maybe we should-" Danahlia stops as does the tiny mouse girl in front of her. Nestled in the heart of the brightest emberstones, these glowing like fires with no smoke, are what look to be eggs. They're easily as big if not bigger than

Alice's head. They appear to have overlapping scales over much of their more tapered ends giving them some rigidity, but the other ends look leathery, not like bird eggs at all. Fortunately or unfortunately, whatever was in them has already hatched.

"Oh wow, what do ya think laid these?" Danahlia exclaims, crouching over them.

"Somethin' big," says Alice, leaning over Twinkaleni to look.

Kaliska stoops over one and looks inside the hollow shell, "Aww, we missed the babies."

Prodding an egg, Danahlia says, "Looks like these've been here a while. Probably for the best, mommas do not like strangers pokin' around their nests."

Twinkaleni falls to her knees as if in reverence. "This is amazing," she gasps.

"Yeah, these are pretty wags," says Alice, picking up one of the empty eggs to feel it. The shell is thick and surprisingly heavy. The scales on one end are very smooth and hard, while the leathery part is tough but pliable. It looks like all the young popped out of the leathery ends. Alice puts it up to her nose and sniffs the inside. It smells awful, like the rotten egg stink of the cavern magnified.

"Do you know what these are?" asks Twinkaleni, examining one of the eggs nearest her. When the others say nothing the Murin spreads her short arms over the nest, "These are dragon's eggs."

Alice's eyes widen at the mention of the mythical behemoths. She, like most others, had been told the stories of how the kingdoms of old were forged by great warriors riding on the backs of dragons. These warriors were revered to be the finest in all of history, as a dragon would only accept the best. From the backs of their fearsome mounts, the dragon riders had brought down the titans that once ruled the world and carved it into the various kingdoms that had since merged into Arsalia.

Danahlia makes a rude noise with her tongue, "No way, there aren't any dragons left in Feoria or Arsalia."

"This seems to prove otherwise," says Twinkaleni, waving a hand over the clutch, "If this female and her brood yet live, well, there could be a handful on this very mountain."

Kaliska has managed to fit two eggs on her hands and now plunges her egg hands through the rest, "Ooo, let's go see them. I bet we can be friends."

"That would be most unwise. Untamed dragons are said to be exceptionally dangerous," points out Twinkaleni, toying with the scales on one egg.

"Oh, hey," exclaims Danahlia, trying to pick up an egg that Kaliska pushed aside. It's too heavy for her at first and she shifts to get a better hold. "Ooo, wow, this one didn't hatch. I could use a dragon egg omelet."

"No!" whines Kaliska, trying to pull it away from the Liguna, despite her hands still being covered.

Danahlia pulls it back from the Chitali, only to have Alice pluck it from her grasp saying, "You can't eat it."

It's quite heavy and warm to the touch but then Danahlia swiftly yanks it away, "Come on, I'm just playin', besides it's probably all rotten any-" She suddenly drops the egg, staring in surprise as it rolls off another to settle once more among the rest.

"What?" asks Alice.

Danahlia watches the egg, open mouthed before saying, "It moved."

About the Author:

K.J. Bailey (Kenichiro Justin Bailey) has thus far only written the Alice Dippleblack series, but looks forward to creating more fantastical worlds.